SINFULLY YOURS

The Five Deadly Sins
Book 4

Kathleen Ayers

Dearest Reader;

Thank you for your support of a small press. At Dragonblade Publishing, we strive to bring you the highest quality Historical Romance from some of the best authors in the business. Without your support, there is no 'us', so we sincerely hope you adore these stories and find some new favorite authors along the way.

Happy Reading!

CEO, Dragonblade Publishing

Additional Dragonblade books by Author Kathleen Ayers

The Five Deadly Sins Series
Sinfully Wed (Book 1)
Sinfully Tempted (Book 2)
Sinfully Mine (Book 3)
Sinfully Yours (Book 4)

The Arrogant Earls Series
Forgetting the Earl (Book 1)
Chasing the Earl (Book 2)
Enticing the Earl (Book 3)
The Haunting of Rose Abbey (Novella)

CHAPTER ONE

MALCOLM SINCLAIR STOOD before the door of the seedy tavern in one of the worst parts of Calais, glaring at the near-toothless man approaching him from behind. He turned with a raised brow at the thief far too stupid to hide the knife in his hand.

"You won't be much good with a broken arm," he whispered to the man in French. "Nor dead." Malcolm cracked his knuckles and slid his coat back to show the pair of pistols tucked close to his waist. "Begone."

The man held up his hands and backed away.

"There's a good lad." Malcolm flung open the tavern door, nose wincing at the host of unpleasant smells assaulting his nose, but grateful for the warmth.

The weather had turned and the icy wind coming off the sea had Malcolm shoving his fingers into his coat pockets. The air in Venice had been far warmer. The city deadly, but beautiful. The port of Calais seemed dismal and dirty in comparison, but Malcolm didn't plan on staying in France.

He hated France.

Roaming about the Continent after leaving the service of his country and selling his commission—some speculated that he'd been dishonorably discharged, which was not the case—Malcolm was at last ready to return home. Lieutenant Major Lind, his commanding officer, had merely *suggested* that England would be better off were Malcolm to end his military career. The duel and three fistfights had nothing at all to do with the officer's opinion.

Malcolm had wanted to return home for some time. Not to Dunnings, that barren estate where his family had been banished for so long, but London. His terrible half-brother, Bentley, had died, not painfully enough in Malcolm's opinion, and his brother, Jordan, had inherited their father's title. Now Lord Emerson, but still impoverished thanks to Bentley bankrupting the estate with is lavish lifestyle and assorted mistresses, the family would be in need of funds. Drew played cards and dice to supplement the Sinclair income, Tamsin raced her horse, Jordan raised pigs. Malcolm became a soldier. Aurora, the youngest, had once grown cabbage and parsnips at Dunnings but now that she was to become a lady and make her debut, he was sure she wasn't digging in the dirt anymore. But money would be needed to launch Aurora into society.

The point being, Malcolm still needed to do his part.

No longer a soldier and without the pay that came with it, Malcolm decided the role of mercenary, seemed a good choice. He lacked any other skills besides a decent sword arm and his marksmanship with a pistol. After spending the last few years being shot at, stabbed, nearly garroted and suffering at least two broken noses in fistfights, the allure of a mercenary life had faded. He'd become a dock worker or a blacksmith if necessary. Better than being awoken with a knife at your throat.

Easier said than done.

Squinting at the dim, smoky interior of *Le Baleine*, Malcolm observed the array of shabby looking sailors, fishermen and smugglers, all drowning their sorrows in whatever sort of alcohol the shoddy tavern offered. Dozens of eyes glared back at him as he walked inside, the door slamming shut behind him. All sizing him up. Trying to determine if Malcolm's size and hardened exterior hid a purse filled with gold.

It did not. Malcolm's gold had already been stolen.

Two days ago, he had gone down the stairs of the Derand

boarding house to search out his breakfast, only to find his landlord, Monsieur Derand slumped over a table, bubbles of white spittle at his mouth and *quite dead*.

Madame Derand entered the room minutes later and began screaming that the *anglais sauvage* had poisoned her husband.

Malcolm tried to explain, in a logical manner, that he possessed pistols and knives. Monsieur Derand had clearly been poisoned.

Madame Derand paused in her screaming, looked him in the eye and murmured. "A woman's weapon, my apologies, Sinclair," before she started screaming once more.

Bitch.

Malcolm had run up the stairs, pushed aside the lone maid the Derand's employed and shut the door to his tiny room. Madame Derand's screams would bring the authorities and he was moments away from being whisked away to some foul French prison for the murder of Monsieur Derand. Convenient for Madame Derand. Once in his room, he went right to the loose board in the floor beneath his bed and nearly screamed as loud as Madame Derand.

The purse, stuffed full of gold coin, most of which he meant to give to his brother once he returned to England, was gone. The maid he'd only just passed, a wren-like thing who had never met his eye, seemed the likely culprit. Malcolm stared at that empty hole, knowing that he had no way to pay for speedy passage to England. The streets of Calais seemed safer than being accused of murder, so he'd fled. Shivering and cold as he wandered the streets, staying to the shadows, Malcolm had shoved his hands in his pockets, the edge of one finger touching the small card he'd been given on his first day in Calais.

Fortuitous.

The card was why Malcolm was here, pushing through the crowd of unwashed bodies, stepping over what looked like a large bloodstain on the floor. A rough, barrel-chested man, eyes narrowed to slits spit, narrowing missing the toe of Malcolm's boot.

"Good thing you missed," Malcolm growled. "Harder to miss my blade."

The man scowled but turned away, wise enough to recognize a much more dangerous predator than himself had entered the tavern.

Good. He really didn't want to kill anyone tonight unless absolutely necessary.

Doing the dirty work of the Venetian doge had been exciting at first, just as soldiering had been. He'd become an expert marksman while in the service of his country, putting bullets into those who more or less deserved it. But such an existence weighed on him. Eventually, Malcolm would find himself on the wrong side of a sword or pistol, and he longed for something much more peaceful. He wasn't sure what he would do once he returned to England, but it would not involve kidnapping, murder, or assassination of any kind.

But fate, it seemed, had other plans.

Malcolm peered through the smokey room and caught a flash of crimson edged in silver. A carefully coiffed head of hair.

For God's sake, why didn't Buckmore just put a sign around his neck asking to be robbed?

Sighing, he pushed past a group of seedy looking men who eyed Buckmore as if he were the largest piece of roast on a dinner plate.

The assignment the young lord offered was distasteful and something Malcolm had promised never to do again, but given his current circumstances, he was in no position to refuse. Payment for the errand was substantial and it included passage to England. Tonight.

Buckmore was one of the Venetian doge's acquaintances, a self-indulged nitwit with more cravats than sense. He'd been in Venice last year enjoying the whirlwind of parties and poisonings, the Venetians did love their poisons, around the time that Malcolm had successfully kidnapped the young lady that the doge wished to wed.

Not his finest moment, though both the doge and the woman insisted it was a love match. Her family disagreed. Strongly. Thus, Malcolm's employer requested her kidnapping.

Malcolm had not seen Buckmore again until a few days ago. The young lord had been wandering about Calais and within moments of reacquainting himself with Malcolm, Buckmore had asked his assistance on a small errand, much like what he'd done for the doge.

Lord Buckmore sat at a corner table, a bored look on his boyish features, drumming his fingers. Conspicuous as only an Englishman in a seedy tavern in Calais could be. The nitwit was practically begging to have his body tossed off the wharf after being picked clean by the sharks already circling him. He was an easy mark, arrogant in his belief no one would dare accost him, with lines of dissipation crossing his cheeks despite his youth. It was doubtful, Malcolm thought taking in the baron's slender form, that Buckmore had the strength to even lift a sword to protect himself. Or hold a pistol.

Buckmore reminded Malcolm quite a bit of Bentley.

He took the seat across from Buckmore, making sure the butt of his pistols flashed briefly from inside his coat to deter anyone from interrupting the conversation. Necessary, with Buckmore flashing about the dim interior of the tavern like a shiny gemstone.

"My lord." Malcolm tossed his saddlebag, the only thing he'd escaped the Derand boarding house with, onto the floor by his feet. There wasn't much in it. Most of his things had been taken along with his gold, save a somewhat clean shirt and a pair of socks. He had never harmed a woman in his life, but thought he'd make an exception for Madame Derand and her maid.

"Captain Sinclair."

"Just Sinclair will do."

Buckmore nodded. "As you wish. I am happy you reconsidered my offer of employment."

Malcolm's gaze left Buckmore to scan the crowd once more. "It's an *errand*, Buckmore. Temporary in nature. I am not in your employ save for this one small task. It would be best if you remembered that."

"Understood." Buckmore inclined his head, golden curls tumbling artfully over his forehead. "And while you might not believe it to be, I assure you this task is an honorable one." His perfect, patrician nose wrinkled as he took in Malcolm's travel-stained coat. "Just as you rescued Antonia from her family on Giorgio's behalf."

God damn it. "You didn't mention this was a kidnapping."

"Oh, it isn't. More a rescue," Buckmore assured him. "And love is a noble cause, don't you think?"

"There isn't anything honorable about kidnapping."

Buckmore's thin little mouth pursed as if he'd bitten into spoiled meat. He didn't care to have his opinion, or his romantic nature, disparaged.

Little twit.

"Nevertheless." Buckmore gave a flick of his wrist. "A young lady and I wish to be wed. Oh, she is the loveliest creature. Our courtship has been nothing short of blissful. My intentions and affection for her are returned."

"Then why do you need me?" Malcolm sat back. "Let me guess, your little dove's family doesn't approve of you. You want me to kidnap this young lady, I take it. I don't do that sort of thing anymore."

Buckmore's lips shriveled to a sharp point. "I don't believe you are in a position to refuse me, Sinclair." A smug gleam entered his eyes. "Are you? I heard about your little problem, though I'm not sure why you would poison your landlord." At Malcolm's look he said, "I grew tired of hoping you'd contact me and sought you out. I was there when they hauled poor Monsieur Derand away. Terrible business, poison."

"I didn't kill him."

"Oh, I'm certain you did not. You're much more a knife and

pistol sort of gentleman. But it doesn't matter what I think, does it?" The fingers drummed once more as his mouth loosened into a grin. "I've already arranged your passage to Dover, Sinclair. The ship leaves on the morning tide, but you can go onboard as soon as our business is concluded. Unless you wish to remain in Calais and find yourself in chains tomorrow. One little errand for me and you can put all this nastiness behind you."

Little prick.

"I assure you this is less an abduction and more a rescue of Miss Brooks from her family. She is in complete agreement."

Malcolm's fingers, covered with scars and callouses, stretched across the table, considering whether he should just toss Buckmore and his damned errand through the window and take his chances with the authorities. His hands were not those of a gentleman, or the son and brother of an earl. But those of man who had done distasteful things in order to survive.

One last errand for this pampered little shit and Malcolm would be that man no longer.

The last letter Malcolm had received from Jordan said that the family was settled at Emerson House in London. Bentley had left a great deal of debt, and Jordan would need to wed an heiress to prop up the family fortunes as soon as possible. Tamsin had also written, pleading with Malcolm to return home in time for Aurora's launch into society. He assumed from both letters that every pound would be needed to give his little sister the life she deserved as a lady, and to help Jordan dig the Sinclairs out of the hole Bentley had left them in. Malcolm had little choice, what with a murder charge hanging over his head and his carefully saved purse of gold gone.

"Fine," Malcolm hissed.

"Splendid." Buckmore sat back and pushed the bottle of brandy on the table in Malcolm's direction.

"I prefer whiskey. Bushmill's to be exact."

"How provincial. I do hope you take heart in knowing that Miss Elizabeth Brooks and I will forever be in your debt. I have been forced into this situation, no matter how abhorrent I find it." He sniffed. "As I said, our courtship was blissful until it was ended abruptly."

"Her family doesn't like you, that much is clear." Malcolm could understand. He didn't care for Buckmore either.

Buckmore's mouth twitched before smoothing out once more. "Mr. Brooks was ready to accept my proposal for Elizabeth's hand. He welcomed my courtship of his daughter." A grimace crossed his lips. "Until her horrid cousin saw fit to stick her nose into the situation. She is to blame for me having to resort to less savory methods to win the hand of Miss Brooks."

"Her cousin?"

"The odious Miss *Alyss* Brooks. A priggish, sour spinster who loves nothing so much as the misery of others. She can't bear to see Elizabeth happy and wed to me. You've never met such a controlling woman."

"I'm sure I haven't."

"Unfortunately, Miss Alyss Brooks wields a great deal of influence with her uncle," Buckmore said in a bitter tone.

Good God, the young baron was dramatic. "How did you manage to incur such dislike?" Buckmore was a pompous gnat. Annoyance probably followed moments after speaking to him.

"As I said, she is a sour old spinster. Unattractive. A self-proclaimed arbiter of all that is proper and moral. She has styled herself as Elizabeth's champion as well as companion. Her age and generally unpleasant personality make the idea of any gentleman finding her the least attractive to be impossible. Strident and cutting. Never a kind word or look comes from Miss Alyss Brooks."

"She sounds quite the shrew." Whatever her unpleasant feelings for Buckmore, Malcolm's were tenfold.

"You've no idea, Sinclair. This is entirely her fault, my having to seek you out and basically abduct the woman I love. I only mean to keep Elizabeth for a night, possibly two. Then we will return to London, and I will officially do the honorable thing. As I said, it is unfortunate Alyss has forced me into this position."

"Miss Elizabeth Brooks is in agreement with being compromised and forced to wed?"

Buckmore flinched. A tiny tic, but Malcolm caught it.

"I do not think this is what she prefers, but all will be handled with the utmost discretion," he said. "No one will know. We can be wed properly before God and London once Mr. Brooks accepts my proposal. I know it would be easier if I simply took Elizabeth to Scotland, for instance. But that would ultimately shame her, something I have no desire to do. We have not been able to speak or even communicate since Mr. Brooks declined to allow our courtship to go further. Alyss makes sure every note or gift I send does not reach my beloved." Buckmore raised his chin.

"How clever, my lord."

Once ruined, Mr. Brooks would have little choice but to accept Buckmore for his daughter or risk her reputation. If Buckmore eloped with Miss Brooks, her father might well take legal action or dispute the marriage.

"There is nothing else I can do because of Alyss's interference. Elizabeth understands things must be done this way," he insisted. "I assure you. She is in agreement."

Not the entire truth. Oh, he didn't doubt that Buckmore had convinced Elizabeth into believing that as star-crossed lovers, there was no other choice but to allow him to ruin her so that they could wed. But he found it unlikely that Miss Alyss Brooks and her opinion of Buckmore was the sole reason Mr. Brooks must have an inkling that Buckmore's devotion to his daughter was questionable. Buckmore's true love was likely the dowry of Miss Brooks.

Malcolm didn't trust Buckmore and his tale of the two Miss Brooks. The more he listened to the young man across from him, the more certain he became that this little errand was one he didn't want.

But he had to leave France. Immediately.

"Payment?" Malcolm asked.

"As I said, I've already purchased your passage. The *Annie May* sits at the end of the dock. The rest upon completion of the task. Once onboard, I'll slip you a purse for your expenses. You'll need to stay out of sight upon arriving in England. I must insist you do not contact your family until after you've completed my errand. The Sinclairs have already caused a bit of an uproar in London, I don't care to become part of it were anyone to know of our association."

He dearly wanted to punch the little prick.

"Mr. Brooks is close acquaintances with Lord Curchon." Buckmore paused as if that should mean something to Malcolm.

Malcolm shrugged. "I'm not sure how that is relevant."

Buckmore's eyes widened just slightly, the only indication that he knew something Malcolm did not about Lord Curchon. "I—suppose it is not," Buckmore said smoothly. "Still, I must insist. Did I ever tell you I was acquainted with the previous Lord Emerson? Terrible about his accident. You have my condolences."

"Yes," Malcolm growled. "A terrible tragedy." Bentley would not have survived much past Malcolm's long overdue return to England at any rate, but the twit sitting across from him didn't need to know that.

Buckmore slid a small sheaf of folded papers at Malcolm. "Notes on Elizabeth and her habits. She likes to walk in Hyde Park every morning. Early. When few people are about. I thought that a perfect time to—*find* her. There won't be any witnesses save her cousin, Alyss."

"How will I know which girl is Elizabeth?"

"Don't worry," Buckmore assured him. "The two look nothing alike. Elizabeth is beautiful, stunning, actually. Like a rosebud about to unfurl." Buckmore sighed. "Alyss, more a wizened apple one has discarded. You can't possibly mistake them."

Malcolm hadn't been to London in years, since before he left for the Continent. He wasn't familiar with Hyde Park. Not anymore. But he'd figure it out. He tucked the papers inside his coat.

"I included the address of the Brooks home for informational purposes only. Mr. Brooks is prominent and influential in political circles. And as I've mentioned, he is a confidant of Lord Curchon." Buckmore again hesitated. "Who is the uncle of the Duke of Ware." A very pointed look this time. "For that reason, I'd advise you to stay clear of the Brooks residence, so you aren't seen."

"I don't know the Duke of Ware or Lord Curchon," Malcolm grumbled.

Buckmore looked away.

"You seem overly concerned I might come across either man. I've been gone from England for some time. The names mean nothing to me. And unless they are walking through the park with Miss Brooks, don't matter."

A sly smile crossed Buckmore's lips. "I thought your brother might have mentioned him in a letter. Due to his prominence in society."

Another lie, but Malcolm was past caring. He only wanted to complete the task before him and return to his family.

"I won't acknowledge you on the *Annie May*," Buckmore advised him. "It would be best if we pretended not to know each other."

Malcolm wished he'd never set eyes on Buckmore and would take great pleasure in not having to speak to him further. "I'll study your notes. Make some observations."

"Send word to me at my club when you are ready. I've put that in your notes. Be mindful of Miss Alyss Brooks. She always carries a parasol which she uses to swat away any gentleman who shows the slightest interest in her cousin. I, myself, have been on the receiving end. Quite unpleasant. She bruised my arm."

"I believe I can handle one shriveled spinster holding a parasol," Malcolm informed him as he stood. Buckmore was such a bloody fop. "We should leave together, my lord," he said scanning the room. "I'd like to make sure we both reach the *Annie May* safely."

"Agreed." Buckmore's gaze swiveled about the tavern. "Though I don't believe anyone would dare accost me."

Malcolm kicked a bundle of rags that had been moving close to their table out of the way, satisfied when he heard a grunt of pain. "Of course not, my lord."

CHAPTER TWO

M ISS ALYSS BROOKS smoothed down the green sprigged muslin of her dress, absently striking at the tall grass along the side of the path with her parasol. The parasol was deceptively draped in lace and ribbons to give the appearance of frivolity. A useful accessory for keeping the sun from one's cheeks.

And loathsome, despicable rakes from innocent young ladies. Liberties were stopped by just the swat of the parasol. Or a poke in the posterior. Alyss had absolutely no compunction about using it to dissuade her cousin, Elizabeth's, amorous suitors.

"It is only that you do not understand Buckmore," Elizabeth sighed wistfully.

Dear God. Especially Lord Buckmore. "I understand him perfectly well."

"He is not as dreadful as you believe, Alyss." Longing spilled from her words as the weak morning sun brushed her porcelain cheeks with a hint of gold. Elizabeth looked like a goddess wandering about the park. Was it any wonder every gentleman in London was half in love with her?

The substantial dowry attached to her skirts only enhanced her attractiveness.

She rolled her eyes. "You are a hopeless romantic, I think." Alyss didn't have the least illusion concerning love or romance, both of which she deftly avoided. Love led one to make poor decisions which often resulted in unwelcome circumstances.

Death being one.

"Buckmore's affections are honest and true." Elizabeth pouted.

Yes, as true as his need for her cousin's substantial dowry.

Buckmore was rapidly spending his inheritance and would be impoverished in less than a year. Alyss had made inquiries after he started to pursue Elizabeth, just as she had on her cousin's other suitors.

"Papa liked Lord Buckmore. Or at least," she frowned. "He did." She shot an accusatory look at Alyss.

"Buckmore took you to a secluded portion of the terrace at Lady Atwood's fete which, if you had been discovered by anyone but me, would have resulted in your ruination."

Uncle Richard was entirely grateful for Alyss's assistance. She served as Elizabeth's chaperone and companion. Her protector. Once he knew of the incident at Lady Atwood's, and Buckmore's lavish spending habits along with other, more sensitive information provided by Alyss, he had no problem declining Buckmore's suit.

"He was stealing a kiss, nothing more," Elizabeth insisted.

"Hmm." Buckmore had been charming his way beneath Elizabeth's skirts and into the Brooks's front parlor with the fervor one usually only saw in hungry mongrels. He'd been refused by two other young ladies, both heiresses, and moved on to Elizabeth. After a detailed review of his character, Alyss had merely presented Uncle Richard with her findings.

"You behave as if Buckmore has committed some great crime."

"I don't find his intentions toward you to be honorable."

Debt, a great deal of it, had accumulated around Buckmore's booted feet in a woefully short amount of time. Not inherited, mind you, which would be somewhat acceptable. A gentleman couldn't be held accountable for debt he'd inherited, for instance. But Buckmore's fault lay in his inept handling of financial matters, his needless wagering on horses and cards and his lavish, self-indulged lifestyle. Art. Sculptures. Horses. Mistresses. Buckmore spent as if he were as wealthy as the queen.

He was not.

Once, he'd taken Elizabeth and Alyss on a lavish picnic just outside of London in the tiny hamlet of Gerryhill. Not nearly as romantic as it sounded.

"He wants to wed me, what could be more honorable than that?"

Two carriages. Six footmen. An entire folly constructed behind a cottage Buckmore owned—which Alyss later found out he kept one of his mistresses in—for that day alone. Not to mention enough food to feed two households.

Overly extravagant in Alyss's opinion.

If her sweet, naïve cousin were to wed him, she and Buckmore would be poor within a year and begging funds from Uncle Richard. Also, Elizabeth wasn't really in love with Buckmore, merely dazzled by his good looks and charm, both of which he had in abundance. Her cousin *claimed* Buckmore to be her great love, but she'd also said that about three other gentlemen in the last few months. Since Uncle Richard refused to allow Buckmore to court Elizabeth further, the cad had attempted to compromise Elizabeth at least twice in addition to the incident on Lady Atwood's terrace, both efforts thankfully thwarted by Alyss.

She took a great deal of satisfaction in besting Buckmore. Scurrilous fop.

"Buckmore is not so bad as you make him out to be."

No, he was far worse.

"You must admit, he is terribly handsome."

"I admit that he is terrible."

Elizabeth pinched her and took the parasol from Alyss. "It is only that you do not believe in love."

"Untrue. I believe in love for you at the very least. But I've never wanted such a thing for me, Elizabeth. I'm quite happy remaining unwed and by now, I'm far too old to be considered good wife material. Possibly at some point I'll engage in a dalliance," she batted her eyes at Elizabeth. "If only to see what the fuss is about."

"Alyss." Elizabeth gasped in pretended outrage. She opened the parasol and tilted it above her shoulder, protecting her cheeks from the sun. "Possibly you'll fall in love one day. What then?"

"I do not think that a grand romance is in my future, Elizabeth. I shall be quite content to remain as I am. Frankly, I think I would prefer a dog rather than a husband. They're much less selfish." Alyss toyed with the locket at her throat, forcing back a host of unpleasant memories. "Besides, I promised your father I would watch over you until you're wed."

"Or Father marries Mrs. Hitchcock." Elizabeth twirled the parasol above her head. "Even I am not so naïve to assume they are merely acquaintances."

Mrs. Hitchcock was the plump widow who lived three houses down from the Brooks' home. She was a lovely woman who came by for tea and a game of whist with her uncle. Though Alyss thought they did more than play cards.

"Perhaps you might reconsider Mr. Clinton, Alyss. He is older. Mature. Well-read. I'm sure if you took the time, you might find him interesting."

Alyss grimaced. There was nothing the least intriguing about Mr. Ronald Clinton aside from his need to wear an enormous mustache. "I doubt it."

Uncle Richard had become acquainted with Mr. Clinton over brandies at the home of Lord Curchon, a close friend of her uncle's. Clinton's enormous, quivering mustache, the very first thing you noticed about him, trembled as if it were alive with each word he spoke. Crumbs and other trapped debris would spill from the carefully trimmed, but voluminous, mound of hair to sprinkle the front of his coat during polite conversation. She found it horrifying, what might nest in all that facial hair.

"He has expressed great admiration for you."

"Yes, all while a bit of scone hung precariously at the corner of his mouth." Alyss couldn't keep the distaste from her words.

"As I said, I think dogs make far better companions at my age than men. Besides, you are only in your first Season and will require my company for some time. After you are properly wed, I may decide to take up painting."

"You've little talent." Elizabeth scoffed. "You do not wield a brush well, only a parasol. At least, Mr. Hammersmith found that to be true."

"Indeed." Mr. Hammersmith, ancient lecher, attempted to leer down Elizabeth's bodice at a function just last week. Alyss struck the tip of her parasol into his foot.

"Someday you will no longer have me to protect, Alyss. Then what will you do?"

"I fear that day is a long way off. But I think I should like a small cottage somewhere in the country. Perhaps by the sea. A home all my own. A place I've no desire to wander from." Alyss had never even lived in a proper house until she'd come to stay with Uncle Richard and Elizabeth. She'd grown up on a stretch of desert. Her father had delighted in dragging Alyss and her mother about with nothing but a tent to shelter them from the elements. Now she longed for a sense of permanence. A home that didn't need to be picked up and carried about on the back of a camel. Or one that truly belonged to her. Elizabeth couldn't possibly understand.

Alyss reached up to grab her locket once more. The rush of old anger at her father receded as soon as she touched the smooth oval of gold. Mama wouldn't want Alyss to carry such bitterness but to forgive Nolan Brooks.

"My virtue is in no danger, Alyss. You're merely overprotective. Especially about Buckmore."

"I disagree."

Alyss had overheard Buckmore at Gunter's only yesterday, boasting to a table of his cronies that he would soon "bag" his "darling peahen," as he referred to Elizabeth, while he shoveled an ice into his mouth. She had to restrain herself from swatting him in the head with her parasol.

Thank goodness Elizabeth had not been with her.

Elizabeth was sweet. Innocent. Kind. More lovely than a spring day. Buckmore only appreciated her for her looks and dowry, nothing else. During their brief courtship he'd spoken to her in a patronizing tone, often mocking her intelligence under the guise of teasing, which Alyss found intolerable. Under no circumstances could Buckmore have Elizabeth, no matter how hard he tried to compromise her.

"The sun has grown warm." Her cousin looked up at the dappled light coming through the trees. "Do you need your parasol?"

"There aren't any disreputable young gentlemen attempting liberties, so no."

Elizabeth burst into laughter. "Oh, I don't know. That shrub over there is giving me a lascivious look."

Alyss chuckled softly before bending to pluck a white flower with a smile. The area around her feet was covered in them. Snowdrops. "I see you," she addressed the snowdrops, loud enough for Elizabeth to hear. "Stop making eyes at my cousin."

Elizabeth whipped the open parasol about, dancing on the other side of the path, her laughter floating in the air. She spun about, revealing trim ankles beneath her skirt.

Well, what did it matter? Alyss decided not to chastise her. There was no one here to see.

CHAPTER THREE

M ALCOLM STOOD BEHIND the trunk of a large maple, breath misting in the early morning as he watched the two women lingering about a cluster of small white flowers, giggling at each other. He'd observed them at a discreet distance since their arrival in the park after following their carriage from the Brooks residence. The driver was already half-asleep, not paying the least attention and the carriage parked some distance from where they walked. No maid or groom accompanied them. And just as Buckmore had said, this area of the park was deserted due to the early hour.

It was unlikely anyone would witness the abduction of Miss Brooks.

There was one small problem. Aside from proclaiming Elizabeth Brooks a great beauty, and decrying Miss Alyss Brooks as plain, with an unsightly, mannish form and the face of a gelding according to Buckmore's extensive notes, he had said little else other than Malcolm couldn't possibly mistake one girl for the other.

The bloody idiot.

The women were of like height. Both slender, though one Miss Brooks dressed in green, had a lovely, curved bottom when she bent to observe the white flowers at her feet. Bonnets, tied around their chins in ribbons matching their dresses, made it impossible to discern their features. Malcolm didn't dare get any closer and risk scaring them off or alerting the driver.

The Miss Brooks in blue spun about, skirts fluttering about her ankles. She held a parasol over her head, occasionally mimicking dance steps and twirling the accessory about. Miss Brooks in green laughed at her antics while plucking a handful of white flowers. Daisies, possibly, though Malcolm didn't think it the right season for daisies.

"Turn around and show your face," he hissed. The least Buckmore could have done was provide Malcolm with a telescope.

A half hour had gone by, and he still didn't know which of the two girls was Elizabeth. The errand had already been delayed by nearly a week, since neither young lady had left the house due to several days of rain. Today, with the sun shining, though there were dark clouds on the horizon, Malcolm decided it *must* be today. He might not get another chance. Word had been sent to Buckmore. The baron had sent a plain black conveyance with a driver, paid for, but declined to come himself, stating he couldn't afford to be seen if things didn't go as planned. The carriage sat just over a small hill to Malcolm's left.

Bloody Buckmore.

Malcolm had already decided that if Miss Elizabeth Brooks balked in the least at her abduction, he would explain the entire affair Buckmore's doing. If the young lady still objected, he would put her back where he'd found her. Buckmore had only advanced Malcolm a small sum on board the *Annie May*, barely enough for a bed, a bath, and a bottle of whiskey. If things went astray, he was unlikely to ask for Malcolm to repay him. Mutually assured discretion between them was in place.

A burst of laughter came from the Miss Brooks dressed in blue. She hefted the parasol over her shoulder as if carrying a rifle and marched like a soldier, down the path. The second Miss Brooks, in green, strolled lazily behind her.

"Dammit." His gaze ran between the two.

Nothing could ever be easy.

Now that he was in London, Malcolm wanted desperately to see his family. He didn't care about Lord Curchon or why Buckmore thought it so bloody important to avoid the man. The lure of the house of Bruton Street tugged at him. There was a portrait of his parents there that he dearly wanted to see once more. Hopefully Bentley hadn't sold it.

But he'd promised Buckmore he wouldn't, not until this task was complete.

God, I hate abductions.

Miss Brooks in blue continued to march about with the parasol, before pointing it at Miss Brooks in green like a rapier.

Wait. What was it Buckmore had said?

"She always carries a parasol which she uses to swat away any gentleman who gets close to her cousin."

Malcolm hadn't paid much attention to the comment at the time, assuming Buckmore to be merely a dandy who couldn't even throw a punch, but—

Miss Brooks in blue put the parasol back on her shoulder. "I am Captain Major Alyss," she said, the words catching on the breeze blowing through Malcolm's hair. "I am here to defend your virtue from those vicious snowdrops." Both girls burst into peals of laughter.

The girl in blue *had* to be Alyss Brooks by her own admission. And she had the bloody parasol. That meant Miss Brooks in green was his quarry.

Malcolm straightened. He scanned the immediate area once more, satisfied that no one else was lingering about. Given her slight build, the easiest thing to do would be for Malcolm to sprint up behind Miss Brooks in green and simply toss her over his shoulder. Quick and fast. Just like a sack of grain. Miss Brooks in blue, Alyss, might scream, but there wasn't anyone to hear. If she fought or struggled, Malcolm would explain that Buckmore had sent him, and if Miss Brooks in green balked, even slightly, he meant to place her on her feet and depart. If she was unwilling, Malcolm wouldn't take her no matter his agreement with

Buckmore.

Once in the waiting carriage, if all went well, the ride from London to Gerryhill, where Buckmore waited, would take just under two hours. He'd deliver Miss Brooks to her future husband and be on his way to Emerson House with a sack of gold.

Miss Brooks straightened from her perusal of the flowers, the skirts of her dress billowing about her trim figure.

Miss Brooks in blue—*Alyss* the dreadful cousin—was closer than Malcolm would have liked, but it couldn't be avoided.

It was now or never.

He took a slow breath, focusing on Miss Elizabeth Brooks, the green of her skirts and nothing else. This wouldn't be difficult when compared to other errands he'd done. How hard could it be to take one woman? Malcolm slowed his breathing, listening to every sound: chirping birds, the laughter of the two women, the silence surrounding them in the park. There was nothing else.

Bursting out from behind the trunk of the tree Malcolm sprinted towards Miss Brooks in green, making sure the handkerchief he'd tied around his face and the brim of his hat hid his features. It wouldn't do for horrible cousin Alyss Brooks to be able to describe him later.

He ran along the line of trees, darting in and out until he was nearly alongside her, focused on her back and the fluttering of her green skirts.

The other Miss Brooks in blue, Alyss, turned abruptly at his approach, her mouth gaping open in shock as she caught sight of Malcolm streaking towards them. She snapped the parasol shut and Miss Brooks in green took it from her hand.

"If you didn't care to hold it any longer—whatever is wrong?" Malcolm heard the slender form in green say to her cousin just as his arms circled her small waist.

The breath whooshed out of her lungs as he grabbed her.

She didn't struggle, instead she twisted, jabbing the end of the parasol into Malcolm's thigh, narrowly missing an important part of his anatomy. His arms wrapped around her like a steel band, prohibiting her from moving further before he hefted her over his shoulder.

Miss Brooks in blue, the cousin, screamed bloody murder and waved her arms about helplessly. "Help! Someone please help!"

"You blackguard." She managed to get one arm free. *Whack.* "Release me this instant." *Whack. Whack.*

Buckmore hadn't exaggerated. Being swatted by a parasol wasn't the least pleasant even though it was made of nothing but silk and lace. "Calm yourself, Miss Brooks," Malcolm growled. "I am here at the request of Lord Buckmore. I mean you no harm."

Whack. This time against his posterior, though since she was thrown over his shoulder, he supposed that was all she could reach. "Buckmore?" Her voice was muffled against the back of his coat.

"Yes. Lord Buckmore."

Miss Brooks stilled immediately. Not another peep came from her, although her cousin was spinning about the path and shrieking as if she'd been the one taken.

He didn't dare stop.

Miss Brooks bounced along his shoulder, still clinging to the parasol. She said not a word as he raced up the hill to Buckmore's carriage, which confirmed to Malcolm that Buckmore had told him the truth. Miss Brooks agreed with her future husband's methods and was more than willing to be compromised so they could be wed. Upon reaching the carriage, Malcolm set her down and caught a flash of delicate features and dark eyes before he lifted her inside. Nodding to Buckmore's driver, he climbed inside to take the seat across from Miss Brooks.

"Go." He rapped his fist on the roof of the carriage.

CHAPTER FOUR

THE REINS SNAPPED and the carriage lurched forward at breakneck speed, rolling out of the park and into the streets, which were nearly deserted at this time of the morning. No one would see them leave, and even if they did, the carriage looked like dozens of others, plain and black with no identifying marks.

Miss Brooks lay in a tangle of skirts on the seat across from Malcolm. She struggled to come to a seated position, her half-boot catching Malcolm in the shin. The parasol swept before him nearly taking out his left eye. Finally, she smoothed her skirts and placed the parasol in her lap to regard him. She had the most unusual eyes. Pitch black, the pupils barely discernable and set against the pale porcelain of her skin.

Something tingled at the base of Malcolm's neck. A warning he'd learned long ago not to ignore.

"Miss Brooks." He rubbed his shin, annoyed, attempting to discern if her well-placed kick had been accidental or not. "I am taking you to Lord Buckmore. You've nothing to fear."

"Oh, I don't know, sir." Her tone was crisp. Tart. Decidedly not as sweet as Buckmore had led Malcolm to believe. "I find being abducted by a complete stranger while walking in the park to be a rather terrifying experience."

Except Miss Brooks didn't seem the least distressed. Or remotely terrified. In fact, she appeared overly calm.

Malcolm's neck prickled once more as the carriage flew

through the streets. They were on the very outskirts of town now and barreling into the countryside.

The bonnet had done an adequate job of hiding her features in the park, but now that Malcolm sat across from her, he studied the sharp but delicate lines of her cheeks presided over by those startling eyes. Her brows were so light as to be nearly invisible against her skin. Her mouth, rich and plump, lips a dark pink, stood out against her stark features. Malcolm had trouble looking away. It was a most interesting mouth, though at the moment, it was pursed in dislike.

"And you could be lying to me. Perhaps you've taken me for a nefarious purpose, using Lord Buckmore's name as a ploy to gain my confidence."

"A nefarious purpose?" Buckmore had said Elizabeth was sweet, but not overly intelligent. He'd never mentioned she spoke like the governess Malcolm had once shared with his brother Drew shortly before their banishment to Dunnings.

A deep breath pushed her bosom up against the confines of her dress as her fingers gripped the parasol. "Ransom, for one. My—" she hesitated for just a moment. "Father is Mr. Richard Brooks and well-known."

So that was her concern. "I assure you, Miss Brooks that I have collected you—

A tiny snort came from her.

"On behalf of Lord Buckmore. He explained the difficulties in your courtship, mainly caused by the overzealous efforts of your cousin. The solution might seem drastic, but his lordship has only your well-being and safety in mind." Malcolm schooled his features into politeness. He hadn't spoken in such a manner since he'd been a child, the courteous speech he'd been taught returning as if it had never left no matter the years he'd been gone from society.

Miss Wallingford, the governess, had been good for something other than being the object of his boyish fantasies.

"I see. How kind of Lord Buckmore to take matters into his own hands." A gloved fingertip gracefully tapped on the edge of the parasol. He'd expected—well, some sort of girlish trepidation. Or giggling excitement filled with romantic prose about Buckmore. Not this eerie calm.

The scent of lilacs drifted towards Malcolm from the direction of Miss Brooks, a wholly feminine aroma that made him think of a warm summer day. One spent lying in the grass while staring up at the clouds above. He hadn't done so since he was a boy at River Crest, his family's estate. There were lilacs in the gardens there, one of his mother's favorites.

"I suppose I should be flattered." Those ripe, luscious lips moved. "That Buckmore went to such lengths to make me his wife. You mentioned Gerryhill?"

"Lord Buckmore awaits you."

"I am familiar. He has a cottage there." She bit into that plump bottom lip.

Malcolm inhaled slowly, his head swimming with the scent of lilacs, eyes stricken at the sight of her mouth. No wonder Buckmore was enamored. Courtesans didn't have lips as fine as Miss Brooks.

"A picnic," those lips moved seductively as she spoke, "was our purpose in being there. A welcome distraction from London. He had a folly built on the property for just that occasion, hoping to impress me. Roasted capon, wheels of cheese, a vast assortment of other delicacies."

Malcolm rolled his eyes. Of course, Buckmore had built a bloody folly and he could care less what this twit and Buckmore had eaten on their picnic. He didn't hate the countryside nearly as much as his brother Drew, but the idea of looking at cows and making polite conversation while nibbling away at a bit of cheese didn't sound the least entertaining.

"You are pleased with the turn of events," Malcolm stated.

"Incredibly. Being compromised by Buckmore so that my father will allow us to wed is what I've longed for. What a brilliant way to circumvent Alyss. That's my cousin. She doesn't care for Buckmore." Her chin lifted slightly. "Will you take that handkerchief from your face? I confess I would be far more comfortable if you did so."

Malcolm had meant to keep his face hidden for the entire journey, but since Miss Brooks seemed, if not exactly thrilled, but somewhat happy that Buckmore planned to compromise her, it didn't seem a huge risk. She was unlikely, once wed, to concern herself with Malcolm. Besides, he hadn't properly shaved in weeks, something he wouldn't do until this task was finished. She was unlikely to recognize him later.

He pulled the handkerchief away from his heavily bearded jaw.

Miss Brooks and her too shrewd eyes took him in. "Do you have a name?" Her fingers tightened on the parasol. "I ask purely out of politeness. If I were to see you again, perhaps at my wedding to Lord Buckmore, I should like to greet you properly."

"I doubt we'll see each other after today, Miss Brooks. My name isn't important."

The lips pursed and rippled at his answer.

Malcolm had the inclination to take that bold, full lower lip between his teeth. Nibble and suck on it. He jerked his gaze away and studied the passing countryside. Innocent, sweet young ladies weren't usually to his taste. Not even if they had a mouth meant to take a man's—

The carriage careened around a corner, jostling them both about.

Miss Brooks grabbed the edge of the window, and uttered a soft curse, the sound of which sent a rush of sensation around Malcolm's mid-section. He wondered what sort of sounds she'd make in bed with that mouth.

What the hell is wrong with me?

It hadn't been that long since he'd been with a woman, but even if it had been years, that was no excuse to lust after an innocent girl who would soon be Buckmore's wife.

"How much longer until we reach Gerryhill?" she murmured.

"We are more than halfway there. Another hour at most."

"Oh good," she said, those curiously dark eyes snapping at him. "I can't wait to see Buckmore."

CHAPTER FIVE

ALYSS TIGHTENED HER hands on the parasol and observed her kidnapper. She had the inclination to swat at him again, but that would likely make him suspicious. Elizabeth would never hit a man, even if he had abducted her. She'd probably be chatting away this criminal while waxing poetic about that wretched cur, Buckmore.

The mere thought of saying anything kind about Buckmore had bitterness flooding her mouth. Foul, disgusting fop.

The dislike of Buckmore was so intense, Alyss nearly snapped the parasol sitting on her lap. But that would defeat her purpose and expose her identity. She couldn't risk that man across from her instructing the driver to turn the carriage. Not when they were closer to Gerryhill than London.

She studied her abductor.

Big, or at least larger across the chest and arms than most of the gentlemen who crowded into the parties and balls she'd attended. He'd picked Alyss up and sprinted across the park, reaching he carriage without so much as stopping to catch his breath.

Alyss supposed villainous abductors must be physically fit.

Slightly disheveled. Unkept. His coat was missing two buttons and there was a tear at the shoulder. He looked as if he slept in the streets or somewhere less welcoming, though no unpleasant odor came from him. When he carried Alyss like a sack of grain she'd caught a whiff of soap, not refuse and horse.

"It's rude to stare, Miss Brooks."

She did not look away or acknowledge his comment.

He did possess an overabundance of facial hair, but she wasn't certain that was by choice, likely more necessity. When a man is busy abducting young ladies, pausing to shave would be a waste of time. At any rate, Alyss didn't care for a mustache on a man, case in point, Mr. Clinton. But not shaving so that your face wasn't discernable behind a wealth of hair made as good a disguise as any.

"So, you are from London?" She needed as much information as possible to provide a good description to the authorities.

He gave her a bland look as sunlight streamed through the window, drawing out the color of his eyes.

A flutter occurred in her stomach. Green, like a freshly picked sprig of mint.

Miss Brooks shrugged. "I was merely making conversation. We still have some time together and I'm growing bored." She pouted as she imagined Elizabeth would have done.

That sharp gaze fell to Alyss's mouth, riveted as if she were speaking of something important. Another flutter, this one pushing along the confines of her ribs, had her fingers sliding over the parasol.

Goodness. He regarded her quite savagely.

"I don't think it important. Where I'm from." There was a gravelly quality to his words as if he'd just woken up. But there were hints of the north in his accent, which was far too posh at times to be that of an ordinary mercenary.

"Very well. It is only that you are far too courteous to have come from St. Giles or Cheapside and your manner of speaking suggests you're from London. It is the accent I can't place." She tilted her head. "I assume you are a former soldier."

His eyes widened just a tad enough to tell Alyss she was correct. "Am I?"

"The way you sit. Carry yourself. The set of your shoulders."

He stayed perfectly still except for one raised brow. "Quite clever, aren't you, Miss Brooks."

"I like to think I am. I'm not fond of mustaches." She nodded at him. "Nor beards of such density. Makes me wonder if a bird could be nesting within."

"Lucky for you, Miss Brooks, Lord Buckmore is clean shaven. At your preference, I'm certain."

Alyss opened to refute the statement, say that she couldn't care what Buckmore looked like, but remembered she was supposed to be Elizabeth. "I can't wait to see my dear Buckmore." The sickly-sweet words tumbled out of her. "Does your family know what you do for a living?" she asked abruptly, hoping to throw him off balance and blurt out some information she could give the authorities. He would probably cut his hair, which was overly long and shave after depositing her with Buckmore, which would completely alter his appearance.

Except for the eyes.

Only jungle cats and the tiny lizards she'd once trapped in the desert had eyes that color.

"I'm sure you are anxious to be reunited with Lord Buckmore," he countered. "After the tragedy of being kept apart for so long. Your cousin sounds quite the termagant if you'll forgive me for saying. Buckmore doesn't care for her in the least." He leaned slightly forward. "Told me she had the face of a gelding."

Alyss inhaled sharply. She knew she wasn't considered beautiful, not like Elizabeth. Or pretty, not with her odd coloring. Hair an ashy blonde, nearly washed of all color. Skin so pale that only a moment in the sun had her cheeks pinking. Eyes like pitch and much too big for her face. But she did not resemble a horse.

"A gelding. Goodness," her voice took on a hint of sarcasm though she tried to stop it. "Buckmore does have a way with words."

"He does, doesn't he?" Her kidnapper sat back. "He also said your cousin was sour. Strident. A terrible prig. No wonder she's a spinster." He shrugged.

"Perhaps she prefers to remain unwed." Alyss looked out the window at the passing countryside. They were very near Gerryhill.

He laughed, showing a line of even teeth. "Doubtful. She probably can't stand to see you happy, Miss Brooks."

HOW INTERESTING. ONLY the very tip of her nose reddened at his insults, that glorious mouth firmly shut into a tight line.

"I think all Alyss wants is my happiness. She may be overprotective of me, but she only wants what is best."

"Or she has designs on Buckmore herself," Malcolm added, purely to see how far he could goad her.

The slender fingers lifted the parasol just slightly off her lap before setting it down once more, as if she'd wanted to poke him with the damned thing but thought better of it.

Miss *Alyss* Brooks was quite something.

Malcolm had figured out her game, and been amused by it, halfway to Gerryhill. That prickling at the base of his neck was rarely wrong. He might have discovered sooner, had Buckmore's description of Alyss not been colored by his obvious dislike. The woman before him wasn't beautiful, not in the way his sister Tamsin was, for instance. But she was striking. Arresting with those bits of onyx for eyes against her fair coloring. And that mouth—

What he couldn't discern was her reasoning for pretending to be Elizabeth, though he eventually concluded it was to confront Buckmore.

Malcolm recalled the younger man's smug arrogance in that filthy tavern in Calais. Buckmore deserved to have his perfect plan ruined, *after* Malcolm received his gold. So, he didn't ask the driver to turn back to London. He'd had little entertainment as of late and this was sure to be amusing.

"She detests him." Her chin tilted in a mutinous manner, toying with the tiny oval of a locket around her throat.

The coldly crisp words, coming from her luscious mouth, sent a wave of arousal twisting around Malcolm's legs.

"Is that a gift from Lord Buckmore?" he said, purely to see how far he could push her before she admitted to her deceit.

"No." Her fingers fell from her throat, drumming along the edges of the parasol once more.

Malcolm peered out the window. "We should be at Gerryhill momentarily. I'm sure you're quite anxious to be reunited with Lord Buckmore, Miss Brooks."

"You can't possibly imagine," she drawled. "I desire nothing more than to see his dear face."

The clipped tone grew more precise. Honed like the edge of a blade.

Malcolm imagined her begging him to take her in that same authoritative tone while running her nails down his back.

Bloody hell. He shifted against the leather seats.

The attraction to Miss Alyss Brooks was as intense as it was unwelcome. Nothing would come of it, of course. But his cock didn't know that.

Malcolm took a deep breath and turned to the passing countryside. Focused on the gold he'd soon have in hand and the upcoming reunion with his family. He did not want to consider *the* Miss Brooks seated across from him, nor the sounds she might make as he bedded her.

The fathomless pools of pitch watched him from across the carriage as if Miss Brooks knew exactly what Malcolm was thinking.

Damn this errand and damn Buckmore.

CHAPTER SIX

NOT LONDON, EXACTLY. Nor Yorkshire. More...Northumberland. There was a gentle roll of Scots in his words which told Alyss he'd lived near the Scottish border at some point. That could be useful information in his eventual capture. Uncle Richard's housekeeper was from Newcastle and the man across from her had the same cadence of speech as Mrs. Duncan. She'd tried to keep him talking, but he wasn't exactly a sparkling conversationalist, not that he could possess much intelligence if he'd gotten himself involved with Buckmore.

Or mistaking her for Elizabeth.

Once he got a good look at her in the carriage, he should have realized his mistake. Buckmore had probably described Elizabeth as beautiful, and Alyss was...*not*. Possibly the man across from her didn't have good eyesight. Which made her wonder how he actually made his living as a mercenary—didn't such an occupation require attention to detail? The aiming of a pistol, for instance, must require keen eyesight. Maybe the man across from her wasn't really good at kidnapping, only desperate and the best mercenary Buckmore had been able to afford.

Ah, Buckmore. Alyss hoped he liked surprises.

If she didn't stop him, confront his outlandish actions today, Buckmore might only do something more ridiculous in the future. He needed to know that Elizabeth would never, under any circumstances, be his. Buckmore should find another heiress.

Vile cur.

Alyss saw his plan clearly. First, Buckmore had Elizabeth abducted, but not by him, so no one would see them together and cause talk. He'd want to show how much he cared for Elizabeth by not deliberately ruining her reputation. Second, Buckmore requested to have Elizabeth taken to a remote location, Gerryhill. Buckmore had a cottage there, as Alyss already knew. He meant to keep Elizabeth there for the night, perhaps longer, then bring her back to London. Elizabeth would confess she was ruined and in love with Buckmore. The scurrilous baron would offer to do the honorable thing, but no one else need know. Her uncle would have little choice but to agree to their marriage, not with Elizabeth ruined and looking as if she'd run straight into Buckmore's arms. Not if he didn't want his daughter to become the source of gossip in London for the foreseeable future.

Blackmail. That's what this was.

Horrid pestilence. Buckmore was worse than the pox.

Well, *she*, Alyss Brooks, would put a stop to this nonsense today. Buckmore was the lowest sort of human being, manipulating Elizabeth's emotions for his own gain. She'd known the moment she'd caught sight of him at a ball; she couldn't remember whose ball, exactly. He'd been deep in his cups, smelling of brandy, but still capable of weaving a spell with his charm and dashing good looks. Alyss watched with contempt as he ushered several young ladies out to the terrace, then returned to the ballroom to brag of his conquests.

Depraved dandy.

Alyss was going to enjoy putting Buckmore in his place.

"We're nearly there, Miss Brooks." Something calculated and knowing gleamed in the depths of her abductor's eyes. His gaze lingered over her mouth once more before returning to the window.

The flutter stretched from beneath Alyss's ribcage to a low spot in her belly, unsettling her to no end. It had been some time since she'd been attracted to any gentleman and she would not start with Buckmore's hired thug.

"Northumberland," she said clearly.

He turned his chin in her direction. "What about it?" But the corner of his mouth twitched at her guess and Alyss knew she was right. He didn't immediately look away, instead, he studied her so intently, taking in the rise and fall of her bosom, that a flush started up her cheeks.

Alyss had never been *assessed*—with such intensity before. She wasn't that interesting. The look he gave her was quite *lascivious*. He was—ogling her bosom and mouth.

"Stop that, this instant," she finally snapped, feeling the blood pulsing beneath her skin.

"I've no idea what you mean," he replied in a bored tone.

"Lord Buckmore would not appreciate your perusal of my person."

A derisive sound came from him before he said solemnly, "My apologies, Miss Brooks."

Alyss's grip on the parasol was so tight she feared she might snap the slender handle. The scenery outside rapidly became familiar to her. She recalled the gnarled oak laying on its side from her last trip here for that stupid picnic. The two small shops, smithy and a stable, which constituted Gerryhill. Farms and sheep dotted the hills in the distance, but there was no one else on the road. No wonder Buckmore had chosen this location. There was nothing here. Gerryhill was a place one passed through, not a destination.

Elizabeth probably would have swooned had she been here, thinking the entire affair to be romantic rather than a desperate grab to secure her dowry. She would think herself a fair maiden in one of the lurid novels she liked to read. And Buckmore the hero.

Not the villain he actually was.

Her cousin deserved better, or at the very least, not to be wed by a man who, once in charge of her dowry, would ignore her in favor of his mistress. He would spend every farthing, secure in the knowledge that Uncle Richard wouldn't allow his only child to starve or go without.

Alyss was *saving* Elizabeth.

This was a noble cause.

The carriage slowed as Buckmore's cottage came into view. Set back a distance from the road, surrounded by pastoral landscape, the small residence was quaint, secluded, and with the wisteria curled around the stone, absolutely the sort of place a dreamy young girl would consent to lose her virtue in.

Damn Buckmore.

On Alyss's last visit, for the picnic, he claimed to use the cottage as a retreat for artistic pursuits, like painting.

She doubted Buckmore even knew what an unframed canvas looked like.

The young lord had once kept a mistress here as well as one in town. A quiet place that wasn't too far from London so that when the mood took him, Buckmore could ride out for the day and be back in time for his evening amusements. The carriage pulled up around the circular drive but no one came out of the cottage. The last time Alyss had been here a caretaker had greeted Buckmore, but she saw no sign of the elderly man now.

"We've arrived," Alyss said unnecessarily to her traveling companion.

"I can see that," he said.

She shrugged. "I didn't take you for being overly observant." Poor of her to say so, but clearly, he wasn't, and now it was far too late for him to return her to London. Even if he did manage to take note of her words.

"You're very certain you can dictate to the world, aren't you, Miss Brooks."

Alyss didn't reply; instead, she scanned the area around the cottage for any sign of that frivolous fop. "I don't see Lord Buckmore."

The carriage halted and a grunt sounded from across the

carriage as her kidnapper leaned over to open the door. She started to move but he put a hand on her arm.

A jolt traveled over Alyss's body at his touch.

"Stay here, Miss Brooks."

"Please hurry," Alyss tried to sound breathless. "I find myself overcome with emotion at the thought of my sweet Buckmore."

"Oh, I'm certain you are." His mouth twitched on one side, a half-smile, as if they shared a joke, just the two of them.

For a brief moment, Alyss considered he might know she was not Elizabeth, but how could he? She'd restrained herself the entire journey, not once allowing her hatred of Buckmore to shine through. Been polite when she wanted nothing more than to swat her captor with the end of her parasol.

And as previously noted, her abductor was simply not that observant.

Banishing such thoughts, Alyss instead concentrated on the mounting anticipation of confronting Buckmore. The look on his handsome features when he realized Alyss had duped him would be *priceless*. Worth enduring the ride to Gerryhill with a taciturn mercenary.

Buckmore would be furious, but there was little he could do.

Alyss did spare a thought for how she would return to London. Buckmore might not be willing to return her. She meant to implore the driver of this conveyance who would certainly not strand a woman so far from town. If that ploy wasn't successful, Alyss thought there would be someone in Gerryhill who would be willing to drive her to London for a price. A handful of coins sat in the reticule dangling from her wrist, a few pounds that she'd taken at the last minute this morning, hoping to coax Elizabeth into a bit of shopping after their walk.

And there was also Buckmore's elderly caretaker. Surely, he would help her if no one else would. She had merely to find him.

Her abductor jumped out of the carriage, the vehicle rocking from his weight, and shut the door behind him.

Alyss could see little out the window other than the cottage's front door. Everything looked as it had on her previous visit. What was the name of Buckmore's caretaker? She strained to recall the man's name, but reasoned the smithy or someone at the stables would know his name and where to find him. There couldn't be too many elderly caretakers in Gerryhill.

Buckmore appeared at the side of the cottage, perfectly dressed in a tailored coat of deep indigo. Boots so shiny they reflected the sunlight, or what little was left at the approach of a line of dark clouds. There was satisfaction stamped clearly on his handsome features as his lips took on an arrogant smirk.

I will wipe that smile off his face.

In his hands he carried an enormous bouquet of wildflowers tied with a ribbon. Buckmore had probably picked them himself from the field behind the cottage, hoping Elizabeth would find it romantic.

Repulsive toad

"Ho. Sinclair."

The broad shoulders standing just outside the carriage window tensed.

So that was her abductor's name, Sinclair.

Sinclair.

Why did that seem so familiar?

Alyss's gaze roamed over the broad back in what was once a decent coat but now worn from travel. Sinclair was a common enough name. But hadn't Alyss heard the name Sinclair bandied about recently? At the charity tea, the one she'd attended in the company of Mrs. Hitchcock. There had been a Lady Longwood at the table beside them, sneering over someone named Sinclair. Or had it been St. Clair?

Good lord, Alyss. It doesn't signify.

"She's inside," the rough voice, slightly patrician but with a hint of the north, said.

Buckmore hurried forward. "Payment first. As we agreed." Sinclair's broad palm pressed against Buckmore's chest, keeping the young lord from drawing closer.

Buckmore tried to shake him off, but Sinclair was several inches taller and considering the way his worn coat stretched, didn't pad himself in the shoulders the way Alyss suspected Buckmore did. Alyss took in Sinclair's stance, the thighs heavy with muscle, and pressed her fingers into the handle of the parasol as a delicious quiver trailed down her spine. She stared a bit longer, unable to look away.

I must give a proper description to the constable.

Buckmore turned his head and cooed, "Elizabeth, my sweet. I'm here, my darling. Don't be frightened." He glanced at Sinclair. "If you touched a hair on her head—"

Sinclair snorted. "I did not. As you said, she's quite biddable." His eyes glinted in the direction of the carriage. "The gentlest of creatures."

Alyss gritted her teeth, surprise flickering in her chest. He *did* know she wasn't Elizabeth.

"My fee." He poked Buckmore none too gently.

"Unhand me. I am a gentleman. I am good for the sum owed." He wavered, glancing at the carriage. "I don't have the amount on my person at the moment. It would be unwise for me to travel about with that much gold. But I promise you full payment once Elizabeth and I are wed. A few weeks at most. Now, get out of my way."

"Isn't that convenient. I doubt, my lord, you had any intention of paying me at all, did you?"

Buckmore's cheeks flushed. "I think not stranding you indefinitely in France should more than suffice as payment. I assisted you out of a desperate situation. Now, *move.*"

A growl came from the larger man, the sound of a wolf playing with his food before taking a bite. Sinclair could rid the world of Buckmore if he chose to do so, but the lord's arrogance blinded him to the fact. Sinclair tossed a glance towards the carriage window where Alyss sat. The smile on his lips reappeared.

He definitely knows I'm not Elizabeth.

Her heart tripped once. Twice. Would he give her up? Tell

Buckmore that Elizabeth wasn't sitting mere steps away in the carriage? She waited, fingers drumming in agitation on the parasol in her lap. Why had Sinclair been in France? That was curious. But a mercenary could work anywhere, she supposed. Doubtless there was a version of Buckmore in France who needed assistance in kidnapping his future bride.

"We'll call it even, then, my lord," Sinclair said in a friendly tone. "Considering you did get me out of France. Where is your horse?" He glanced at the trees surrounding the cottage. "The one I was promised use of?"

Buckmore was so bloody full of himself. So confident that Sinclair had acquiesced because...well, he was Lord Buckmore. Not even honorable enough to pay the kidnapper he'd hired. Alyss wanted to burst into peals of laughter but didn't dare. Not yet.

"The stable you passed on the way through Gerryhill is where you'll find the horse. I've informed the groom there who you are and what to do."

Sinclair stared at the younger man for a space, but ultimately nodded. He walked in the direction of Gerryhill but then paused and crossed his arms, looking at the carriage. The half-smile firmly on his lips. He was rather handsome, standing there even with mud on his boots and despite the overgrown beard.

Alyss's skin hummed a scant second before she reminded herself that Sinclair was a nefarious kidnapper who she would report to the authorities immediately upon her arrival in London. Buckmore would be harder to implicate, simply because he carried a title. But she'd do her best.

Buckmore hurried towards the carriage, pausing only to check his reflection in the window.

Alyss rolled her eyes as she slid back from the door. *Oh, for goodness sake.*

"Don't be shy, dear Elizabeth." He opened the door and thrust out the pathetic bouquet, which now that Alyss got a good look at it, was wilted and half dead.

"You contemptible rake."

Buckmore had only a moment to gasp at the sight of Alyss before she launched herself out of the carriage. Driving the end of the parasol into Buckmore's stomach, she next swung about and whacked him on the backside, just as she'd been longing to do for weeks.

"Surprised to see me? Loathsome creature," Alyss hissed.

Sinclair stood some distance away, watching but not interfering. His chest moved slightly as if he were trying not to laugh aloud.

Buckmore made a terrible wheezing sound as the parasol made contact with his soft stomach. "You—where is Elizabeth? What have you done with her?"

Alyss swatted him on the shoulder and jabbed him once more in the stomach as he held his arms up to deflect the blows. "Blackguard. Vile despoiler of young women."

Whack. Whack. Whack.

"You bloody *idiot*." Buckmore screeched at Sinclair dropping the bouquet as Alyss chased him around the carriage. "This isn't Elizabeth." He looked up at his driver. "This is not Elizabeth Brooks."

The driver shrugged. "I didn't know which girl he put in there, my lord. He told me to go, and I did."

Alyss pointed the parasol at Buckmore, forcing him backward.

"This," the baron screamed at Sinclair, red-faced. "Is *Alyss*." The coward ran to hide behind the man who'd abducted Alyss from the park. "I told you Elizabeth was beautiful. Are you blind? How on earth could you mistake the two?"

Alyss spun about raising the parasol once more, aiming it in the direction of Sinclair, the blood roaring in her ears. Buckmore deserved every swat of her parasol. "Your mistress will be terribly disappointed to find she won't be receiving that ruby necklace after all, Buckmore."

Buckmore's eyes bugged out in shock. "You—were eavesdropping on me. At Lord Harridan's."

"Don't bother to deny it. I believe your exact words were, 'When my dear sweet little nitwit is mine, I plan to give Francesca a necklace of rubies for her patience. The poor dear.'" Alyss swung the parasol over her head. "'Has had to endure only half a proper household staff.'"

Sinclair deftly stepped aside. "I don't believe I am the enemy at present, Miss Brooks. Please direct your parasol elsewhere."

A chuckle came from the driver atop the carriage, which he quickly silenced at Buckmore's quelling glare.

"Pardon," she said to Sinclair before stomping towards Buckmore. "You vile, disgusting, *horrid* little lordling." Alyss felt incredibly powerful, a goddess come to life to vanquish Buckmore. "As if I would allow you to trap Elizabeth into a marriage."

The intensity was back in Sinclair's eyes as he took her in. Honestly, why was he still here? Unless he planned to help. "I'll pay you all my pin money if you break his nose."

Buckmore wailed.

Sinclair shook his head. "I don't think you need my help."

"Then be on your way," she snapped at him. His eyes glittered like emeralds as he watched her. So achingly lovely. For a mercenary.

Alyss turned from him, ignoring the sudden unsteady rhythm of her heart because it had nothing to do with Buckmore.

"I will ensure my uncle, indeed all of society, is advised of this entire sordid affair," Alyss declared. "I plan to tell Elizabeth *everything*. Once the word gets out, there isn't an heiress in all of London who will have you, Lord Buckmore. Good luck in your impoverishment."

His handsome features reddened, and the ends of his golden hair stood up like spikes around his ears. "Spoken like the jealous, *unwanted* spinster you are, Miss Brooks." An ugly sneer curled his lips. "God knows, no man would ever wish to kidnap you. Unless they are half-drunk on brandy and unable to see in the darkness." He glared at her.

Alyss flinched.

"Harpy." Swinging open the carriage door, he paused before climbing in. "Good luck finding your way home, Miss Brooks. You aren't welcome in my carriage."

"Cad," Alyss hissed. "You cannot strand me here."

"Of course, I can." A thin smile crossed Buckmore's face, distorting his handsome features. "Meddling, sour thing that you are. I promise you will regret crossing me, Alyss Brooks. Far sooner than you think."

Slamming the door, Buckmore disappeared as the carriage eased out of the yard and onto the road towards London, dust kicking up from the wheels.

Alyss coughed and lowered her parasol. Elizabeth was safe. Her virtue intact. She had exposed Buckmore as an unscrupulous gentleman. It shouldn't be any surprise he was dishonorable enough to not even allow her to sit atop with his driver. Dusting off her skirts, she smiled to herself. It had been *immensely* satisfying to hear the parasol as it made contact with Buckmore. Hopefully, he'd be bruised.

"Did you enjoy the show?" She straightened and shook out her parasol but didn't turn.

Silence greeted her, aside from the rumbling of thunder in the distance.

"One should always ask for their fee up front when dealing with a gentleman such as Buckmore." More silence. When Alyss spun about, she saw that she was completely alone in the small courtyard before Buckmore's cottage.

Another dull crash of thunder met her ears.

Her lips twisted in consternation. Well, what had she expected? Assistance? She suspected Sinclair might have once been a gentleman, but he wasn't any longer given his occupation. He had abducted her in return for payment from Buckmore. He certainly wasn't under any obligation to render aid to his victim.

A small burst of panic filled her chest. She would be fine.

There was a stable attached to the blacksmith only a short

walk away. There had to be a groom or some sort of stableman who would jump at the chance to earn a bit of extra money by taking her to Uncle Richard. If not there, well, there was a small mercantile shop just down from the blacksmith. The proprietor would certainly be able to offer guidance or direct her to Buckmore's caretaker. She'd start there.

Picking up her skirts, grip tightening on the parasol, Alyss set out for Gerryhill.

CHAPTER SEVEN

MALCOLM SHOULD HAVE been utterly furious, but surprisingly, he was not.

The sense that Buckmore wasn't going to pay him for kidnapping Miss Brooks had grown along with the certainty that his traveling companion was Miss *Alyss* Brooks and not her cousin. Buckmore was exactly like Malcolm's older, unloved half-brother. Arrogant and so full of his own self-worth that he assumed everyone else was merely hovering about to do his bidding. He could well see Bentley concocting some half-baked scheme such as this.

All the blame wasn't Buckmore's, however. Malcolm *had* abducted the wrong young lady.

At least he wasn't in France.

Malcolm had to admit, watching Miss Brooks leap out at Buckmore, parasol raised like a charging Hussar, had been magnificent. And given his attraction to her, the single most arousing thing Malcolm had witnessed in some time. It nearly made up for Buckmore refusing to pay him.

He'd felt bad, leaving Miss Brooks to find her own way back to London, but the sooner their association ended, the better. Buckmore, the idiot, had referred to Malcolm by name and sooner or later Miss Brooks was bound to recognize his family. The brother of the Earl of Emerson being accused of kidnapping would light the gossips on fire in London. If he did run into Miss

Brooks again, Malcolm planned on being clean shaven with his upper-crust accent firmly in place and showing nothing of that barren estate in Northumberland that Bentley had banished them all to. Dunnings.

The sky darkened rapidly above him. A storm was coming. And if the line of deep gray, nearly black clouds headed towards Gerryhill was any indication, it would be a bad one. He turned in the direction of the stables attached to the smithy where Buckmore had left a horse for him, catching sight of Buckmore's carriage as it left the small hamlet.

Buckmore had stopped at the stable.

"Bloody hell." Malcolm cursed. "That little prick."

That prickling on his neck returned, the sensation that all was not right. He didn't think payment for kidnapping Miss Brooks the only thing that Buckmore was going to deny him.

Approaching the smithy, he took care to avoid the area where a stream of smoke and steam belched from the entrance and made his way directly to the stables. Gerryhill was small, barely visible on a map with nothing to recommend the tiny hamlet. A perfect spot to ruin a young lady, with no one to see. Buckmore wouldn't want anyone to know he'd compromised Elizabeth, let alone had her kidnapped. He had his own reputation to protect. He'd probably planned a lavish wedding.

Alyss Brooks had ruined all that for Buckmore. Malcolm seriously doubted the little worm had the decency to see her back to London if only to convince Miss Brooks not to say a word. But Miss Brooks, in addition to being sharp-tongued, a bit of a shrew and a know it all, struck Malcolm as highly resourceful.

She'd be fine. And she was no longer Malcolm's problem.

He entered the stables, the smell of manure, hay, and horse assaulting his nostrils. Once his eyes adjusted to the darkness, he could make out a row of stalls. At least three held horses.

A dirty looking man, the stableman, he supposed, sat atop a bale of hay with a knowing look in his eye as Malcolm approached. He smiled, showing a row of uneven teeth stained yellow. A hole in the crotch of the man's trousers revealed most of his questionable assets. "Can I help you?"

"I believe there is a horse waiting for me, courtesy of Lord Buckmore," Malcolm said without preamble. "The name is Sinclair."

The shifty gaze ran flicked over Malcolm. "Huh. No horse I'm aware of. Lord Buckmore ain't been here in some time."

"How odd, I just saw his carriage pulling away."

A bit of straw flicked in Malcolm's direction. "Must be mistaken. His lordship hasn't been around in some time. But lots of carriages look alike." He shrugged. "I have a horse you can have for a price. Or you could walk back to London." He looked up as a rumble of thunder echoed through the stable. "Best decide. Storm's coming."

He had no coin, as this poor excuse for a human being likely knew. Buckmore hadn't paid him. There would be no horse either, though he was certain Buckmore's sat in one of the stalls. Petty of that little lordling, to strand him in Gerryhill for abducting the wrong girl.

"Stealin' a horse is a hanging offense," the man said unnecessarily from his perch on the bale of hay.

"It is, isn't it?" Malcolm contemplated just shooting this bloody idiot and taking Buckmore's horse, but the smithy might come running with his own pistol. The few denizens of Gerryhill would catch sight of him riding away on a stolen horse after shooting one of their own. He could bide his time and return in the wee hours of the morning, slip inside the stable and take the horse. From the smell of gin rolling off the stableman, he probably slept soundly.

"If you're going to walk back to London, you'd best set out now. Next village is Wayburn. There's a tavern. Coach comes through there," he said helpfully with a sly grin. "That's your best bet."

Malcolm inclined his head. "Much appreciated."

He strolled down the road in the direction of London, keenly aware of both the groom and now the smithy watching. Once out of their line of sight, Malcolm doubled back through the woods to Buckmore's cottage, watching as lightning flashed through the trees. The cottage would be stocked with food and probably wine since Buckmore had planned to seduce Elizabeth Brooks. He could ride out the storm in the cottage, drink the little prick's wine and eat his food, then steal the horse just before dawn. He kept to the trees so as not to be seen, pausing on his way only when a slim figure in green, clasping a parasol, came into view on the road, marching with determination in the direction of the stables.

Miss Alyss Brooks. Buckmore *had* stranded her.

Cursing, Malcolm came out onto the road, against his better judgement, and hailed Miss Brooks.

Scowling at the sight of him, she lifted her parasol. Tendrils of white-blonde hair had escaped from beneath the bonnet, probably during the confrontation with Buckmore, and trailed down one cheek. The contrast between her hair, pale skin, and the pitch-black eyes was so vivid, so unusual, Miss Brooks didn't appear to be real.

Malcolm's breath hitched.

Fairy.

A bad-tempered one at that. His mother had once been an actress, one of her great sins, according to society, and a lover of Shakespeare. *A Midsummer Night's Dream* was one of her favorites. Mother had played the part of Queen Titania many times on stage. She adored the stories of the Fair Folk and often would spin tales for Malcolm and his siblings of pixies, fairies, gnomes, and elves. She'd always maintained that since Drew and Malcolm, though twins, looked nothing alike, one must be a changeling. Then she would laugh and smother them in kisses.

A pinch occurred over his heart. He missed his mother.

Mother would have taken one look at Miss Brooks and proclaimed her to be one of the Fair Folk. Alyss's features, though delicate, were comprised of sharp angles. Not beautiful, exactly.

But striking, with a sort of savageness that took your breath away. Buckmore's hatred of Alyss had colored his thoughts on her appearance. Not a bit of it was true.

Miss Brooks poked him in the chest with the tip of her parasol.

"That will be enough nonsense, or I'll snap this frilly thing in half." Malcom wrapped his fingers around the parasol. "I mean it."

Lowering the parasol, she gave him a scathing look. "Out searching for another young lady to kidnap? I think your odds are better in London." Her eyes were so dark, Malcolm couldn't make out the pupils. And that mouth. He barely heard her words because he was so entranced with her lips.

A tiny volley of shocks rippled over his skin. Lust. For this creature.

"You're probably right, Miss Brooks. But then, you're correct about everything." The problem with Miss Brooks, outside of his attraction to her, was that in her own way, she was as arrogant as Buckmore. What other young lady would pretend to be someone else, assault a lord and strand herself in the country, just to prove her point?

Her eyes narrowed.

"Nothing at all in Gerryhill except sheep and you. But," he placed a hand on his chest. "I've already abducted you once today. I don't care to do so again."

"You're quite impertinent for a man facing kidnapping charges. I wonder if you will display the same manner when you are awaiting execution for your crimes." She leaned closer, bringing the scent of lilacs. "Which you will. I plan to study and relay every detail of your appearance."

"Has it occurred to you, Miss Brooks, that you've little in the way of defense should I decide to toss you into the ditch or perhaps trade you to a band of roving highwaymen?" He raised a brow.

God, she was so cantankerous, he did want to toss her in a ditch, if only to raise her skirts and give her a proper tupping. It could only improve her mood.

She placed the parasol over one shoulder. "When did you know, Mr. Sinclair, that I was not my cousin?" The words snapped along Malcolm's skin, crisp and sharp. Tart.

Malcolm enjoyed sour things in general. Lemons. Green apples. Miss Alyss Brooks. He longed to have just one taste of her, though for obvious reasons, that would be unwise. Didn't stop him from thinking of it, though.

"Buckmore described your cousin as sweet. Innocent. A darling." He cocked his head. "It became clear during our conversation in the carriage that you are none of those things." He said the words purely to irritate her.

Her lips pursed into a delicious rosette. "At least I am not a mercenary who abducts young ladies for nefarious purposes."

"Less nefarious, and more a purse of gold coin. And I've never said I am a mercenary."

Another arrogant snort. She would have made an excellent doge in Venice.

"Miss Brooks," Malcolm knew he would regret his next words.

"Absolutely not. I would never accept your assistance. You are worse than Buckmore."

Malcolm had to disagree. "I haven't yet offered to help you," he snapped back.

"You could be planning on holding me for ransom." She gripped the parasol and waved it at him. "Or have other vile plans for me. You are a mercenary. Hired for all manner of unpleasant tasks."

"I had no idea how unpleasant," Malcolm retorted with a pointed look.

"I would never accept assistance from you," she hissed. "I would rather walk back to London where I will promptly visit the authorities to give them a full accounting of today's incident and your description."

"Suit yourself, Miss Brooks."

Annoying little fairy. He was only trying to help, mostly because being around Alyss made his skin tingle as well as another part of his anatomy. But it really would be wise to let her go. She didn't want his help.

"I shall." She lifted the parasol over one shoulder.

"Fine," he uttered.

"Fine." She swished past him, headed straight towards Gerryhill.

Stubborn chit.

Miss Brooks didn't require his protection, her tongue was the only weapon she needed. He hadn't any doubt she'd badger someone in Gerryhill to take her back to London.

ALYSS MARCHED INTO the tiny hamlet, determined to find someone, other than a paid mercenary, to take her back to London. She'd considered offering the bit of coin she had to Sinclair in exchange for his help, such was her desperation, but stopped before she could do so. He was far more likely to simply take her money and disappear. Alyss had only considered it because, well, outside of the abduction, he *had* treated her respectfully. Hadn't hurt Alyss or even really touched her.

Truthfully, he was far less nefarious than Buckmore.

A laugh spilled from her. A mercenary, far less dangerous than foppish Buckmore?

She resolutely put one foot in front of the other.

"I'll start with that tiny shop." Alyss took in the small building on the other side of the stables. "They'll know where I can find that lovely caretaker of Buckmore's."

CHAPTER EIGHT

ALYSS ADJUSTED HER seat, trying to keep her skirts from touching Mr. Elrood. Difficult, because the seat of the gig was narrow and barely large enough for two of them, but still, she made every effort to keep as great a distance as possible between his thigh and hers.

After making inquiries at the small mercantile, Alyss was displeased to find out that Buckmore's caretaker had left the area to live with one of his daughters. When she asked about hiring a gig to take her to London, the shopkeeper pointed Alyss in the direction of the stables. Which was how she came to hire the slightly odorous Mr. Elrood.

Another roll of thunder sounded, and Alyss looked up at the roof of the gig where a decent-sized tear gave her a glimpse of the menacing clouds above them. A strong gust of wind buffeted the vehicle, dispelling some of Mr. Elrood's rather musky smell, for which she was grateful. Goodness, her kidnapper had smelled better. Like cedar and soap with just a hint of horse.

But Alyss didn't dare complain.

The journey to London had already cost her every bit of coin in her reticule, her bonnet, which she'd agreed to hand over before climbing in the gig, and an additional amount to be paid by Uncle Richard upon arrival. The price, nearly three times what the trip should have cost, was because of the weather. Mr. Elrood could find himself unable to return to Gerryhill and might have to seek out accommodations for the night.

She'd agreed, because there was little choice. Alyss couldn't very well spend the night at Gerryhill. There was no inn. No place for a woman of good family to seek out a room. And there wasn't another groom, driver, or anyone else who would be willing to take her to London from Gerryhill. Not with the storm upon them.

Alyss could have gone to Wayburn, the village an hour's walk from Gerryhill. Wayburn had an inn. She could have sent word to her uncle tomorrow morning to fetch her. But time, Alyss sensed, was of the essence. The need to inform her uncle about Buckmore's scheme took on great urgency.

A raindrop hit her nose, falling through the hole in the gig's top. Another drop hit the top of her head, which was no longer covered. What Mr. Elrood meant to do with her smart little bonnet was anyone's guess.

When the gig passed Buckmore's cottage, Alyss was surprised to see smoke curling from the chimney until she realized that Mr. Sinclair had been walking in that direction. He could add burglary to his list of crimes. Hopefully, the next time she saw him would be with a constable in tow. She was grateful he hadn't thought to take her hostage and hold her for ransom to recoup the money promised by Buckmore. Uncle Richard would pay any sum for her safe return.

Her family must be beside themselves with worry. Elizabeth would have gone home and told Uncle Richard what happened. Bow Street runners were doubtless already searching for her. Another reason she must get home as quickly as possible. Once Alyss had her fingers around a steaming cup of tea, she would give Uncle Richard every detail. Buckmore would not escape. Uncle Richard was a member of Lord Curchon's inner circle. Lord Curchon was highly placed in Her Majesty's government. He would make sure Lord Buckmore was punished for his misdeeds.

Alyss wiggled on the seat, though any attempt to make the

ride more comfortable was near impossible. What little padding the seat possessed had long since worn away. There was also the matter of the very odorous Mr. Elrood, whose thigh and leg kept brushing insistently along hers. But the ride, even with the poor weather, should take no more than two hours at most. She could tolerate Mr. Elrood and a bruised bottom for that long.

It had been a most trying day.

Mr. Elrood, thankfully, wasn't one for conversation. His breath was nearly as bad as his body odor and Alyss was happy to spend the journey in silence. Fat dollops of rain started to pound on the roof, leaking through the hole to fall along Alyss's shoulder.

After less than a half hour, with nothing but the rain and her thoughts to occupy her, Mr. Elrood drew back on the reins.

"Why are we stopping?" Alyss asked. "Is it the storm?"

"I'm afraid this is where we part ways, Miss Brooks." Mr. Elrood peered into the gloom. "That bit of coin you gave me was only enough to get you this far. Not all the way to London and certainly not in this rain. I have my horse to think of."

"But you agreed," Alyss sputtered. "You said you would take me to London."

"Yes, but his lordship paid me even more to ensure I did not." Elrood grinned, the stump of one rotted tooth showing just above his bottom lip.

"Buckmore?" She knew he was a total wretch and dishonorable to boot, but to deliberately—

"Now, I'll take that pretty locket, Miss Brooks." Elrood interrupted her thoughts. "And the silver combs in your hair. Maybe that little purse hanging from your wrist. Pretty enough without the coin."

"Lord Buckmore paid you not to take me to London? Why not just refuse at the stable?" She slapped at his hands as they reached for the combs in her hair. "So you could rob me?"

He grabbed at her while Alyss kicked out at him, until the heavy weight of her hair tumbled down her back. "His lordship didn't say I couldn't rob you." Elrood snatched the locket from around her neck, swiftly dumping it into his pocket with the combs. He pulled at her wrist until the reticule came free.

Alyss's hand went to her throat. "Please, not the locket, Mr. Elrood. I'll give you anything else. My half-boots. My petticoats. That locket is all I have left of my mother. It isn't even gold."

"I'm sure she left you good memories." Mr. Elrood's brows lifted. "And gold or not, I bet it still fetches a good price. I hadn't thought of your petticoats." One hand gripped the edge of her skirts. "Or this gown."

She flew at him, pummeling him with her fists. "Get your hands off me." Alyss tried to stab him with her parasol, the only thing she had left, but he grabbed the end. They struggled back and forth until she kicked him hard in the thigh and he released both her and the parasol.

"Bitch." Mr. Elrood unceremoniously pushed her out of the gig.

Alyss gasped as she fell to the ground. A hole, rapidly filling with water and mud, broke most of her fall or she would have been injured. She struggled to get to her feet, pushing wet hair and muck out of her eyes, only for her ankle to roll over a rock and send her back into the mud.

"I'll take that silly umbrella too. It'll be worth something once it's clean." Elrood sneered, making to leap out of the gig.

Alyss pushed aside her sodden skirts and stood, holding the parasol over her head. She'd bludgeon him if he came any closer. "Come and take it. I dare you."

Several minutes passed as they stood glaring at each other while the rain swirled around them. Mud dangled from her hair and skirts. Her half-boots were wet. She was in a sorry state and knew it, but he would not have her parasol.

"Bloody mad. That's what you are." Mr. Elrood sat back down on the bench. "Keep your little umbrella. It's stained with mud anyhow." He snapped the reins and the gig pulled forward. "Stable's back that way." He yelled back at her. "If you start now, you might be there before nightfall. Or you can try for Wayburn. Someone might take pity on you." He spit into the muddy road, narrowly missing her feet as the gig rolled past.

"Bloody, blasted hell."

A crack of thunder sounded above Alyss, followed by a bolt of lightning across the sky, illuminating the muddy road, the windswept trees, and the fact that she was very much alone. Not that Elrood had been the best company. A tiny sob threatened to climb up her throat and Alyss pushed it viciously back down. Adversity was not something Alyss shied away from. She'd had worse happen to her and survived.

Her fingers ran over her now naked throat.

Nor was it the first time she'd lost something dear to her.

Clutching her parasol in one hand, she focused on putting one foot in front of the other. The air had grown colder, and Alyss shivered in her wet clothes.

Buckmore had deliberately stranded her here. Whether out of dislike or something more sinister, Alyss didn't know.

Mama's locket.

She had few possessions she treasured. One of her father's notebooks where he'd recorded a variety of useless facts while dragging her and Mama across the desert. A tiny carving of a snake given to her by one of the guides employed by her father. And Mama's locket. The only thing left of Mary Brooks. Mama had never taken it off. Until—well just until.

That wave of bitterness, most directed at Nolan Brooks, her father, snapped Alyss's spine straighter. Forced her steps to become more resolute. This too would pass. Stranded by a petty lordling whose scheme she'd thwarted wouldn't break her.

Alyss was nothing if not resilient.

Her feet tangled in her skirts, and she stumbled, nearly falling to her knees, but caught herself. She took inventory of her choices, poor though they were.

Obviously, returning to London today was out of the question. Buckmore and the weather had seen to that. But by tomorrow, a farmer or possibly even the smithy might be induced to take her. If not, Alyss could walk to Wayburn and send Uncle Richard a message from there.

But first, she must find a place to get out of the weather. The stable, perhaps, would suffice. Now that Elrood was gone.

Uncle Richard must be beside himself.

How many times had he told Alyss that she must stop attempting to bend the world to her will? That her stubborn nature would one day get her into trouble. Her desire to prove herself correct in nearly every instance.

She supposed allowing herself to be taken in the park this morning would count.

I had to protect Elizabeth.

It was far too late to question her recent choices. Better to focus on recalling every detail about Mr. Elrood. She meant to turn him in to the constable as well as Sinclair. Alyss would have to trust Uncle Richard and Lord Curchon to take care of Buckmore. Her musings made the walk at least somewhat tolerable.

Despite being kidnapped and pushed from a gig in the middle of a muddy road, Alyss wasn't hurt.

That was something.

A gust of wind sailed right through Alyss and her wet clothing nearly knocking her to the ground. Cold rain bit into her skin. But at least it wasn't sand. Nor unbearable sun. Not a chance she would die of thirst.

After nearly an hour, one in which Alyss worried that Elrood had sent her in the wrong direction, she finally caught sight of a warm glow in the darkness emanating from between the trees on one side of the road. A few more steps and Buckmore's cottage took shape. She could smell the smoke of a fire. Alyss tilted her chin forward, forcing herself to walk past and head to the stables at Gerryhill. There only one person who would be at Buckmore's cottage.

But heat. A fire. Perhaps even a blanket. She tried to stretch her fingers but they were numb.

A large, shadowed form moved in front of one of the cottage windows, barely visible through the rain which grew heavier by the moment. And she was so bloody tired.

Alyss took a deep breath and sidestepped a large puddle. Resignation filled her.

If she had to share accommodations tonight with her inept, attractive kidnapper, so be it. Sinclair was unlikely to tell anyone.

And she was far too cold and hungry to care.

CHAPTER NINE

MALCOLM NURSED THE brandy in his hand, wishing it was good Irish whiskey, and threw another log on the fire. The dampness in the air was finally beginning to dispel in Buckmore's little love nest. Only one room, the fire was sufficient to heat the entire cottage. Clean, with the larder and sideboard stocked, Buckmore had obviously taken great pains to prepare the place for his intended seduction of Elizabeth Brooks. When Malcolm had opened the door—very well, he'd picked the lock which wouldn't have put off an infant—he had been surprised to be greeted by the smell of beeswax, clean linen, and a vase of fresh cut flowers.

There was cheese, bread, a crock of butter, a roasted chicken along with a pie, an assortment of apples, potatoes, and some carrots in the larder. Enough for a decent meal. Eggs. There was even a cannister of tea and a pot of honey. The bed boasted a soft mattress. Plenty of blankets. Firewood had been stacked carefully just around the corner.

Truthfully, Malcolm couldn't have found a better place to ride out the storm. Afterwards, he'd retrieve the horse. Buckmore owed him.

How had Miss Brooks fared?

I don't care.

Malcolm pushed thoughts of the vicious little fairy—that's how he thought of her—out of his mind. The attraction to her, though strong, was not enough to cause him to completely disregard every shred of common sense he had to look for her. He was glad his offer of help had been rejected. Miss Brooks was a woman hell-bent upon reporting him to the authorities.

The Sinclairs couldn't tolerate the scandal. Not on top of the dire financial circumstances Bentley had left them in and not with Aurora about to make her debut.

Malcom had seen the shoddy looking gig that passed the cottage some time ago. It had to be Miss Brooks and whomever she'd convinced to take her to London. Probably the surly stableman Malcolm had encountered. The one with the hole in his trousers.

"It isn't any of my affair," he said to the empty cottage, before taking another sip of brandy.

He didn't care for the idea of Miss Brooks having to speak to the stableman, nor endure his company for the length of a ride back into London. Mr. Brooks would ensure the stableman's discretion concerning his niece with some extra coin. And if any lady could handle herself in such a situation, it was Miss Brooks.

Lovely, terrifying creature.

He'd never in his life met any woman bristling with so much righteous indignation. What had made Miss Brooks so prickly? Malcolm judged her to be older than he, perhaps thirty. Definitely a spinster. Any man who had the bad luck to be taken with her striking looks would have to survive her sharp tongue, strong will, and abrasive personality.

Malcolm liked the thought of Miss Brooks purring like a satisfied cat. But only for him.

Not that it mattered. He'd no intention of seeing her again. Far too risky. He had his family to consider. Once he returned to London, he would become Mr. Malcolm Sinclair—he refused to use the rank the military had given him—brother of the Earl of Emerson.

A gentleman.

Malcolm ran a hand through his hair. Once close-cropped,

he'd allowed the thick, walnut-colored strands to grow until they brushed his shoulders. He hadn't shaved in recent memory, the beard covering his face completely hid his features. Working for the doge, it had been best to cultivate a menacing image. That of a dangerous and unpredictable mercenary who would snap your neck if you so much as approached him.

Pity that hadn't worked with Buckmore.

Nor with Miss Brooks, come to think of it.

Still, most people gave him a wide berth. Malcolm possessed a temper, a failing among all the Sinclairs. He and his brothers had brawled since they were children. It was his temper that had ended his military career, but by then, he'd become an expert marksman, good with pistols and swords. Knives as well. He liked to fight. Was good at it. Guarding the doge had seemed a good idea at the time, but no one had warned him how dangerous the job would be. Or how much killing, accidental or not, would be involved.

That sort of thing left a stain on a man's soul. At least as a soldier, Malcolm could tuck those thoughts away as duty to his country. Not in Venice.

What Malcolm wanted most was to control his own destiny and not have his existence be dependent on the whims of his commanding officer or a spoiled Venetian nobleman. A nice little house in the country, like this cottage, but perhaps a bit larger. Maybe some chickens. Unlike his brother Drew, Malcolm did not hate the countryside. Though they did share a hatred of cabbage.

He immediately took another sip of the brandy to dispel the memory of cabbage in his mouth. It had been the only thing to grow at Dunnings. Terrible stuff.

He'd have to learn a trade, which might prove difficult since the only thing he excelled at was weaponry, which made him only suitable for being a soldier or a mercenary. Surely, there was something else he could learn to do. Planning. Strategy. He was good at those things. Picking locks. Breaking into a residence.

Wonderful. He was suited for the life of a criminal. Perhaps

Miss Brooks was correct.

He swallowed the remainder of his glass and poured another, pausing to glance outside at the storm. The wind was whipping through the trees lashing the cottage with waves of rain and debris. If Miss Brooks made it to London before nightfall—

A growl came from him. She was *not* his concern.

Buckmore was probably ensconced in his London home, mulling sourly over the day's events, and decrying the loss of Elizabeth Brooks and her fat dowry, satisfied that at least he'd stranded Malcolm and Miss Brooks. Smug in his assurance that none of what happened today would blow back on him. He'd simply find another heiress.

There he went again. Thinking of Alyss.

Resolving to drink as much of Buckmore's brandy and wine as he could and eat the entire contents of the larder, Malcolm turned to refill his glass when he spotted a figure through the torrent of rain outside, plodding with determination down the muddied road.

"Oh, holy hell," he hissed.

At first glance, Malcolm thought it a wraith. Or a banshee. Or possibly the specter of one of the people whose life he'd ended.

A tiny chill caressed his spine.

In addition to fairies, Mother had also believed strongly in ghosts and other more unpleasant creatures not of this earth. And if anyone deserved to be haunted, it was Malcolm, given the things he'd done.

Tangled ropes of wet hair fell over one shoulder of the mud-stained figure as it moved in the direction of the cottage, not bothering to sidestep the puddle in its path. The figure wobbled as the first step sent a splash of muddy water into the air, struggling to gain a foothold in the puddle before stepping back onto the road. The figure paused, flipping back a dirty strand of hair, before straightening and shaking out the fabric of its skirts.

A whisper of green appeared beneath the layer of muck covering the dress. There was a stick clasped in one hand, also covered in mud.

The remainder of Miss Brooks' parasol.

"Bloody hell."

He'd wondered if today could become any worse, and outside was his answer. Miss Alyss Brooks hadn't managed to get herself to London after all. Setting down the glass in his hand, Malcolm first went to the fire and threw on another log, stoking the flames until they roared. She'd be cold. Hungry. Irritable. She might even hit him with the badly battered parasol she carried.

A zing of anticipation shot through him.

Miss Brooks did not bother to knock, given her current state, he supposed she deemed it unnecessary. Flinging open the door with a bang, she first tossed in her parasol which clattered to the floor. Rain blew in around her as she stepped inside, a clump of mud falling from her skirts with a plop. Pushing the ropes of wet hair from her forehead, she glared at him before kicking the door shut with one foot, nearly losing her balance due to the weight of her skirts.

"Miss Brooks." Malcom didn't dare come any closer. There was murder in those dark eyes.

"Abductor," she addressed him politely.

Malcolm stroked his chin, the warmth he'd felt moments ago spreading over his arms and legs. He couldn't decide if he was pleased or not to see her. Aroused, definitely.

"You're dripping all over the floor."

"Keenly observant, as always," she snarled.

"I saw the gig go by hours ago. I assumed you'd be in London."

"That makes two of us," she snapped. "I'm freezing. I see you availed yourself of Buckmore's cottage. Are you adding burglary to your list of accomplishments?" A shiver took hold of her, teeth chattering as more mud fell from her hem.

"The door was unlocked," he lied. "I thought it best to return to London tomorrow, after the storm."

Miss Brooks made a poofing sound. Defeat and defiance

warred in her features as she looked up at him. "Unbeknownst to me, Mr. Elrood was in the employ of Lord Buckmore."

"Elrood?"

"Yes," Miss Brooks answered. "Disgusting stableman. Owns a tattered gig. Unfortunate hole in his trousers which displays his shortcomings."

Malcolm bit his lip to keep from smiling. "I've made his acquaintance."

"I engaged him to take me to London, but he changed his mind abruptly and left me in the road after taking my things." Her voice trembled for a moment and one hand absently went to her throat, which was now naked with no sign of the locket he'd seen earlier. "But he did not take my parasol."

There was a desolate look in her sharp features at the mention of the locket. He'd observed the necklace earlier. Not fancy. No jewels. But meaningful to Miss Brooks.

"Buckmore stranded you."

"Not once, but twice."

And society in London thought the Sinclairs were savages. "He instructed Elrood to rob you."

"I believe Mr. Elrood came up with that notion all on his own." Miss Brooks waved a hand. "Or at least, Buckmore didn't specifically state not to relieve me of my things. Had I not fallen from the gig, I think it likely he would have taken my petticoats and possibly my dress. I'm sure Buckmore is hoping I've been devoured by wolves."

"There are no wolves in England. Not anymore."

"I know that." She rolled her eyes at him and walked towards the fire, dirty skirts dragging muck across the floor. "I was being flippant." The fight had gone out of her, all the bravado and capability surrounding her earlier had been beaten away by the elements. "Think how desperate I must be to seek sanctuary from my kidnapper. Though at this point, I think it safe to say you might be less dangerous than either Buckmore or Mr. Elrood."

"I never tried to rob you."

"No, you did not. A point in your favor, Mr. Sinclair."

The tugging at Malcolm's insides, like tenterhooks sinking into his flesh, became stronger as he observed Miss Brooks. He wanted to pull her into his arms and shelter her, though he'd never met a woman less in need of coddling. Outwardly, at least.

If he happened to find Elrood sleeping at the stables when Malcolm returned to steal the horse—a low rumble left him. Well, snapping a man's neck didn't require that much effort.

"Don't snarl at me," she stated. "Please. I—As I said, I find I am in need of shelter. You are the only port in this storm, so to speak." Her lips tightened as if the effort to ask for his assistance was more than she could bear. "If you could allow me to stay here and perhaps you might seek shelter in the stable—"

"No," Malcolm stated. "I'm not going to go outside, struggle through a massive wall of water and sleep on a bale of hay, all that so I can satisfy your sense of propriety."

"But it *is* improper—" she straightened her shoulders.

"I find it interesting *that* bothers you more than the fact I abducted you this morning. We were in a carriage alone together for at least two hours."

That delightful, scornful mouth pursed. "Surely you can see that we cannot spend the night in such close quarters together."

"If you feel that strongly, Miss Brooks, feel free to seek out the stable yourself. I'm quite comfortable. There's chicken if you want some." Malcolm picked up his glass and refilled it with brandy.

"But—" She frowned at him. "I demand—"

"You are in no position…" His eyes ran down her bedraggled form. "To demand anything, Miss Brooks. As you keep reminding me, I am nothing more than a lowly kidnapper. A criminal who you hope to report to the authorities. What makes you think I would think I care about your sensibilities? I might just as well toss you back out into the rain."

"This is all your fault," she said stiffly, changing tactics before stretching her hands out before the fire to warm her fingers.

"I think Buckmore and your own arrogance shares some of the blame, Miss Brooks."

An outraged gasp came from her. "I was defending my cousin from a nefarious suitor."

"But you could have accomplished that by announcing who you were before we left London instead of deciding to confront Buckmore yourself. Leaping out of a carriage, brandishing a parasol is not very ladylike, after all."

Her eyes widened. "You—"

"Yes, yes." Malcolm shrugged at her furious glare. "I'm abhorrent. A kidnapper. You could go on for the remainder of the afternoon and most of the night. In fact, I expect you to. But after you change out of those wet things. Behind that screen," he gestured towards the bed dominating the entire far corner of the cottage. "The last thing I need is for you to fall ill, and I am forced to see to your care. Over there is an armoire filled with lots of lace and frills. There should be something you can put on until your clothing dries."

"I will not." She lifted her chin. "The very idea is absurd."

"Fine. Catch your death. Can I offer you a brandy?"

She gave him a wary look from those pitch-colored eyes and shivered once more.

"You are chilled to the bone, Miss Brooks."

"Do not move from this spot." She slowly made her way to the screen, watching Malcolm as if she expected him to pounce.

Miss Brooks and her instincts were not entirely incorrect. The wet, pathetic but proud creature before him had an interesting effect on his cock, especially with her wet dress molded to her slender, but generously curved form. He'd spent an entire day considering what it would be like to have her scream out his name in that bloody, crisp tone while he pleasured her. The image refused to go away.

Without another word, she spun on her heel and stalked to the screen next to the bed. The armoire was flung open. A bit of lace and satin was flung at the bed along with a sound of disgust.

Followed by a pile of satin, also deemed useless. Finally, the noises stopped. Miss Brooks must have found something that suited her. Dirty half-boots were tossed out. Then a pair of stockings were draped over the screen.

Malcolm turned back to the fire and took another swallow of brandy. No sense in torturing himself.

Then the screen rattled. Grunts and the slap of wet fabric met his ears.

He smiled into his glass. Ah yes. The corset.

"Mr. Sinclair," the words bit out.

"Yes, Miss Brooks."

Silence, but Malcolm could sense her fuming behind the screen.

"It appears that while I've managed to relieve myself of the dress, there are other parts of my wardrobe for which—I might require additional assistance. There is no other woman here—"

She sounded as if she would weep.

"And thus, I am forced to request the help of my kidnapper."

"To be fair, I wasn't your kidnapper, Miss Brooks, but your cousin's." Malcolm stalked towards the screen, careful to stop a few feet away. The thought of her pale, delicate skin, just on the other side of the screen, had sensation traveling down between his thighs. His fingers tightened on the glass in his hand.

"What seems to be the issue, Miss Brooks?"

She was silent for some moments. How it must infuriate her to ask him for help, and for such a delicate task. "There is the matter of my corset."

Malcolm set down the glass. "Of course, Miss Brooks."

CHAPTER TEN

ALYSS HAD STEPPED behind the screen in a fit of indignation, horrified to be in a position where not only did she need to seek shelter from her kidnapper, but also had to endure his company for the entire night. Had there been anything at all of a gentleman inside him, Mr. Sinclair would have offered to sleep in the stables. But he was nothing but a criminal. Buckmore's hired help. Albeit handsome as sin behind all that beard with eyes like a jungle cat.

Another shiver struck her, and this time not from her chilled skin.

The reality of the situation was that Mr. Sinclair, mercenary and abductor, was the first and only man who'd ever aroused Alyss in any way. Yes, she'd found gentlemen attractive before and enjoyed their company though few ever made advances in her direction. Now she was about to have a man she'd met only this morning, one who was meant to kidnap her cousin, help her discard her clothing.

And it aroused her.

She placed a hand over her wildly beating heart.

Alyss Brooks was *not* a heroine in a lurid, gothic novel. After spending her childhood in the desert chasing her father's ambitions, living like a nomad and more worried over snake bites than embroidery, Alyss now had the life she'd desired since she was ten years old. No more roaming about on camels. An actual roof over her head. Books. Clothing that wasn't rags. She had embraced manners, rules, and restrictions after the chaotic lifestyle her father thrust upon her. She chaperoned her cousin because it was the least she could do to thank Uncle Richard, who'd lost his wife when Elizabeth was barely a year old. Watching over her cousin allowed Alyss to be part of the social whirl without having to participate. And she knew what it would lead to if she did. Love. Affection. That was a trap for women. Alyss had her place, and she was comfortable.

She would not be her mother who had fallen for a man like Nolan Brooks.

Alyss had accomplished her goal to become a paragon of womanhood. An independent woman. Respectable. One who had a firm grip on herself and those around her.

Launching herself at Lord Buckmore and beating him with a parasol had been a *shocking* loss of control.

The self-control she'd woven about herself since the age of ten had frayed and snapped in places over the course of today. Now faced with spending the night with Sinclair, hungry, cold and with her righteous anger towards Buckmore fading, Alyss felt even more keenly the loss of her usual control. It unsettled her to a great degree.

The armoire just to her left, far too beautiful to be sitting in Buckmore's remote cottage, was filled with a collection of scandalous lacy bits of fabric meant more for seduction than actual sleep. Nothing at all practical. Finally, after sifting through mountains of fluff, Alyss found a nightgown that wasn't sheer. The garment was modestly embellished, with straps made of ribbon. It would have to do.

Her dress had been difficult to get out of, but not impossible. The fabric and buttons were wet, but she could reach them all by twisting about, cursing the entire time that her corset had been laced too tightly.

Oh, bloody hell.

The curse felt right on her tongue, given the situation. Once,

Alyss had cursed with regularity given her upbringing, though she no longer did so. Often, she'd been the only child in the vicinity and no one, including her father, remembered her presence when uttering such vulgarities.

If there was ever a day for such language, it was today.

She had tried to control the situation with Buckmore earlier by allowing herself to be taken instead of Elizabeth. Determined to confront him herself. Now she was stranded in Gerryhill about to ask her abductor to help her out of her corset.

Wise or right, Alyss? I fear you are always determined to be the latter.

Uncle Richard's words lingered in her mind. Today had not been wise.

But I was right about Buckmore.

"Mr. Sinclair." She could sense him just on the other side of the screen which was incredibly poor protection. A whiff of cedar caught in her nostrils as he drew closer. "There is the matter of my corset." Her tone remained authoritative. Crisp. Concise. She didn't even stumble over the word.

"What about your corset, Miss Brooks?"

Wretch. She could hear him smiling. "I find I cannot relieve myself of the garment without some help. Do not attempt to take liberties, Mr. Sinclair." The idea of him touching her, even accidentally, had her breath hitch.

"Miss Brooks," he said in a bored, rumbling tone. "You resemble nothing so much as a drowned rat at present. Wholly unappealing."

"Nevertheless, shut your eyes." A quiver of anticipation ran through her, and she forced it away. This was necessity. Not seduction.

"If my eyes are closed how—" A sound left him. "I'll avert my gaze. I vow to not look upon the sight of your cold, pimply flesh, which will remind me of nothing so much as a fish. Which I do not care for in the least."

"Flattering," Alyss snipped. "Let us hurry things along." She clutched at the sodden fabric of her dress tight to her chest. "I'll assume you understand what must be done."

The brush of his palm settled just above her waist, lingering with infinite slowness up the length of her spine, finger trailing over the edge of the corset. His hand was warm and slightly possessive, demanding her attention. A thumb teased rather impudently at the back of her neck.

Alyss stared straight ahead at the wall before her. He was toying with her, pretending interest he didn't feel to unsettle her further.

"The strings are soaked," he murmured. "Knotted." His voice had lowered to a deep, melodic murmur. "I'll have to cut you out of it."

"Cut me out of it?"

Sinclair leaned over her shoulder, the very edge of his nose brushing along the curve of her ear. "Yes. The strings cannot be undone. I've never understood why women place themselves in such a contraption. How do you even eat properly? Or take a breath?"

"It is necessary."

"I don't think so."

The palm remained at the base of her spine; big fingers stretched out nearly spanning across her back. Alyss hadn't considered, until just now, how much larger Sinclair was than she.

"I once witnessed a young lady in—" he hesitated. "Where I was once employed. Tiny wisp of a thing. Waist unnaturally small. She could barely eat, only a few sips of soup. Fainted dead away before the second course was served."

"I thought you were a mercenary. On what occasion would you have to dine with a young lady in such an environment?"

"I never claimed to be a mercenary, Miss Brooks. That is your assumption. I haven't dissuaded you because you'll fight to the death to be right. And it has been a rather long day." His breath buffeted along her shoulder.

"I am most usually correct about a great number of things."

She shivered again, though not from the cold, but from him being so close. What must Sinclair be thinking, looking down on Alyss, soaked and filthy, her skin pebbling like the skin of a goose? Her earlier reminder for him to not take liberties now seemed foolish. Sinclair found her unappealing, he'd just said so. Compared her to a fairy and she did not think he meant the ones who were vastly beautiful and glowed with starlight. Nevertheless, his light touch startled Alyss greatly. Her pulse fluttered madly about in her throat, unable to stop. No member of the opposite sex had ever been so close to her before. Mr. Clinton sitting next to her on the settee while crumbs sprayed from his gigantic mustache did not count.

"This will only take a moment." His hands fell away, leaving her chilled once more. The sensation of a blade flattening against the corset had her gasp, as did the feel of the laces being sliced away. Alyss took a deep lungful of air at her release, skin prickling as the corset fell away. Sinclair had a point. Corsets were a rather detestable contraption.

A disgruntled sound came at her back. "Your skin is reddened from that thing." His breath fanned once more along her neck, smelling lightly of the brandy he'd been drinking. She didn't dare turn around.

"Then I beg you, do not look further," she answered crisply.

"I wouldn't dream of it, Miss Brooks."

The feel of him, his warmth, fell away, moving to the other side of the screen, filling Alyss with an odd sense of disappointment.

It wasn't as if I wanted him to take liberties.

Moments ago, he had compared her to a fish, and he made a point of adding he didn't care for fish.

Alyss was not blind to her lack of appeal. Looks aside, she *was* difficult. Even Elizabeth, who loved her, claimed that at times Alyss *chafed* a person, as if she were a pair of boots which didn't fit and left blisters.

What does it matter? He is a criminal. My abductor. In league with Buckmore.

Sinclair's heavy tread moved across the cottage. The sound of another log being tossed on the fire met her ears. Her modesty was safe, and she was glad of it.

Yes, for what little good it has done you your entire life.

She released the dress, letting it fall to the floor in a heap. Daring a peek from behind the screen, she saw that Sinclair's back was to her. Quickly she shucked off her layer of wet petticoats, hesitating at her underthings for only a moment before discarding the wet cotton as well. Preserving modesty was one thing, spending the remainder of the day in damp underthings, another. Sinclair had cut off her corset, for goodness' sake, barely touching her. He didn't find her the least attractive. Only wet. Like a fish.

He spent some time studying your mouth in the carriage.

Alyss refused to consider what was only a trick of the light. Fingers trembling, she donned the nightgown she'd found, deftly tying the shoulder straps into bows. She looked down her body, trying to discern if anything was visible. Best not to chance it. She grabbed a blanket from the bed, wrapping it about herself, Alyss was instantly warmer and felt as if she had some sort of protection.

One hand reached up to touch the tangled wet mass of her hair. She must look a fright. Not that she cared what Sinclair thought.

Alyss looked across the bed to a small side table which held a brush and comb. She doubted the pitcher beside them held any water, but there was a towel. Making her way over she dabbed at her face. No mirror, so she had no idea if she'd gotten all the mud from her cheeks.

Another thing she must ask from him.

Taking up the brush and comb, careful to keep the blanket wrapped around her, Alyss made her way past Sinclair, chin lifted, to find a seat before the fire. Unfortunately, the cottage didn't boast an abundance of furniture. Two chairs sat cozily beside each other before a low table. On the other side a settee.

Alyss chose the settee.

"I'll gather your things, Miss Brooks."

"There isn't any need," she said in a rush. She'd been so concerned with her appearance and clinging to the blanket, she'd nearly forgotten her wet, discarded clothing. "I'll—"

"Never let go of the blanket," he finished. "You have it in a death grip. Allow me." He pointed to a bit of twine he'd hung up before the fire on one side.

Alyss looked down. "I'll put down these," she held up the comb and brush. "And return for my things. It isn't necessary."

"I've two sisters, Miss Brooks," Sinclair grumbled. "And I'm aware of what a lady's undergarments look like. I doubt I'll be struck dumb by the sight of yours. And I've just seen you in your corset."

Two sisters. Alyss filed the information away. She pulled the blanket around her shoulders, making sure she was covered from just beneath her chin to her ankles. "You did seem well acquainted with corsets."

Sinclair made a sound of amusement before retrieving Alyss's dress and other more delicate items, carefully placing them over the line he'd strung with his big hands. Handsome features pulled together as he concentrated on hanging everything perfectly. A bloom of heat struck her in the middle of the chest watching him. Would his touch be as gentle?

Horrified at such thoughts, Alyss jerked her gaze back to her lap.

She should be more concerned with how she would explain this entire incident to Uncle Richard, or what details the authorities would most need to apprehend Mr. Elrood, Sinclair and level accusations at Buckmore. Not how it would feel to have those broad palms and fingers caress her body. Yet that was all Alyss could think of. Being touched.

It has been a trying day and I am not myself.

"Buckmore stocked the larder, or someone did," he said,

draping one of Alyss's petticoats over the twine. "There's chicken. Bread. Cheese."

Alyss curled into the settee, tucking the blanket around her body.

"And brandy." He thrust a small glass at her. "Drink. You'll feel better."

"Oh, I don't partake of spirits." The lie came easily from her lips. She did enjoy a glass of brandy now and again, but Alyss thought, given circumstances, she should keep her wits about her.

"You do today. Drink."

His eyes were so impossibly green. Like the first leaves sprouting from a tree at the sign of spring. Sinclair might change everything else about his appearance, but not that.

The glass wiggled before her.

"Very well, for medicinal reasons," she murmured, taking a small sip. The brandy spread across Alyss's stomach, warming her from the inside out.

Sinclair disappeared to the other side of the cottage and moments later, a plate with a roasted chicken leg and sliced apples was placed in her lap.

"You should eat, Miss Brooks. Else you won't have the strength necessary to report me to the authorities. I like brandy. Chicken. I've two sisters and a familiarity with a lady's clothing." The side of his mouth twitched. "Anything need repeating? Should I find paper, so that you can take notes?"

"I'm sure you think yourself amusing."

"Should I growl and threaten you? I can if you wish."

If Alyss didn't know better, and she did, she might assume that Sinclair was … behaving flirtatiously towards her. Very unmercenary-like. Though she'd never once met a mercenary, or any criminal. She had nothing to compare him to.

There was an aristocratic look to Sinclair's features, at least the ones glimpsed behind that burst of beard and mustache. Only the nose gave him away. Broken, at least once if the knot along the bridge was any indication. The flaw only enhanced his attractiveness, adding an element of danger. But if one took away the abundance of facial hair, he would look completely different. Not as old.

"You're younger than I am," she stated with certainty, popping a bit of apple in her mouth. "Though it is difficult to discern your age given your lack of concern over trimming your beard and mustache." She nodded to his hair. "And you're in dire need of a haircut."

"I'm sure you'll include all of that in your recitation of today's events. I'll assume that you took note of Buckmore in the same exacting manner. You probably had him investigated."

Alyss chewed on another piece of the apple, instructing her cheeks not to pink. "Unnecessary. I belong to several charitable organizations. Attend society events while chaperoning my cousin. One has only to listen and observe. It is no great secret that Lord Buckmore once had a substantial inheritance but has wasted a great deal of it on frivolous pursuits."

Sinclair regarded her with interest. "Go on."

She took a defiant sip of the brandy. "His coat, while expensive, shows a fraying at the cuffs. The cravat at his throat, while tied to perfection, is worn through in places though his valet took great pains to hide such wear." Alyss shrugged. "Elizabeth has a large dowry. One that can save him from impoverishment. She is innocent for an heiress and does not realize that Buckmore's designs on her have less to do with affection than her dowry."

"Society is full of impoverished gentlemen. It isn't a crime to wed a girl for her dowry."

"Yes, but Buckmore's nature and self-indulgence is the cause of his poverty. His estate was in fine shape until he inherited."

Sinclair's coat had been discarded, and she took note that he was in nothing but his shirtsleeves. The cuffs were rolled up, showing thick wrists, and forearms dusted with dark hair. There was a smattering of small scars and callouses. The results of handling weapons, no doubt.

"I assume Lord Buckmore promised you a great deal of money he doesn't have to abduct my cousin." Alyss waited for his agreement.

He hesitated a moment, as if trying to consider what he should admit to. "I believe you overheard our conversation when the carriage arrived, Miss Brooks. I think you have all the details." A wave of deep walnut colored hair fell over his brow, and he absently pushed it away before tugging at his beard in annoyance.

"You'll wait, won't you? To shave it." She nodded to his beard. "Until we part ways."

Sinclair's fingers drummed against his thigh.

"You don't need to answer. Your silence is confirmation enough," she said smugly.

"What makes you so sure I won't dispose of you, Miss Brooks?" He purred in her direction. "No one will miss a deranged, parasol wielding spinster from London, will they? So intent on proving yourself correct about Buckmore you are now sitting here, at my mercy."

Alyss bit into another slice of apple. "Only part of your little speech is true. I carry a parasol for the obvious reasons any other woman does."

"So you aren't from London, are you?"

"Nor deranged, no matter what Buckmore told you," she replied stiffly. Engaging Sinclair in conversation had been so that she could ferret out important information about him. But he'd deftly turned the tables.

"Interrogation is only amusing, Miss Brooks, when you are the interrogator, isn't it?"

She looked down at her plate. Perhaps if she offered something of herself, he might be induced to do so in kind.

"I didn't always live in London," Alyss lifted her chin. "I was born there but drifted about until I was ten." There, that would give Mr. Sinclair something to chew on. "You aren't from London either, are you?"

The grin on his face broadened, showing a lovely row of

teeth. Lips far too sensuous for a common criminal. Or a mercenary. She imagined such men as missing part of a limb, with rotted teeth and scars on their face. But even with her abhorrence to facial hair, Alyss found Sinclair to be—

Breathtaking.

Alyss once more looked away, struggling to retain her usual no-nonsense, authoritative manner. Difficult to pretend haughtiness when your wet underthings were dripping water a short distance away.

"I see your game, Miss Brooks. Very well. I spent my childhood in London. Or at least, some of it."

Sinclair came towards the settee where Alyss sat, leafy gaze trailing over her curves neatly hidden by the blanket. He settled himself on the other end, no matter that he hadn't been invited.

"But you grew up elsewhere," she countered.

"Northumberland, near a nondescript village you wouldn't know even if I wished to give you the name. You remind me of my eldest sister. She's overbearing and overprotective as well, though she's never carried a parasol in her life. Possesses a wicked right hook to the detriment of noses everywhere."

"Your sister sounds marvelous."

"Oh, she is." Sinclair refilled his brandy. "She's not," he tapped the bridge of his nose, "responsible for this."

"What is her name? Your sister," Alyss said in a casual tone. When he didn't answer, she said. "You won't tell me because I might recognize her name." She peered at him. "Or your family."

He was looking at her strangely, tilting his head to one side.

"What is it?" She touched her hair belatedly realizing she'd not used the comb. Her conversation with Sinclair had taken precedence. "It's rude to stare."

"A bit of mud on your cheek." He took up a corner of the blanket, pulling it up her body until the edges of her feet and ankles were exposed. Gently, he wiped at her cheek. "Right here."

Alyss froze in shock. Sinclair's face was so close to hers; she could see the tiny bits of gold floating around his pupils. The edge of his beard tickled her chin. A slow, lazy burn of honeyed warmth surged up her limbs as her toes curled.

He sat back an inch, dabbing at her neck. "I was trying to determine what sort of fairy you might be," he rubbed gently at a spot on her neck. "Maybe a brownie of some sort. Or a pixie. All large eyes and terrible teeth."

"You make me sound quite vicious," she whispered.

"I like vicious creatures, Miss Brooks. Where were you drifting about? Before London?"

Alyss didn't speak of her family or her past often, though it was no great secret. But rarely did anyone seem interested. "The desert. In a tent. I doubt you would recall the area even if I named it," she said tartly, reminding him that he hadn't given her the locale of his childhood either. "My father fancied himself a collector of antiquities." She ignored the wave of bitterness that erupted just thinking of Nolan Brooks.

"Perhaps you're a jinn."

Alyss's eyes widened just slightly. "You know what a jinn is?"

Sinclair shrugged. "I find such things interesting." His gaze never left her face, as if Alyss were the most fascinating of creatures. Something stirred inside her, tightening in her midsection and then unfurling across her limbs once more.

"Who told you about such things, Mr. Sinclair?" She wanted to trace the tip of her finger along that knot in his nose.

"My mother." There was such longing in that lone word. So much grief. "She didn't know about jinns, I don't think. But she loved stories of fairies and elves. Pixies. Changelings."

"Changelings?"

"Fairies like to steal human children and replace the infant with one of their own, which soon becomes apparent as the child grows older. A changeling. I don't resemble anyone in my family, not really, thus my mother liked to say I was a changeling."

Perhaps that was what Alyss was. She'd looked nothing like her mother and certainly didn't share her father's passions.

"I don't resemble anyone in my family either," she said, surprising herself. Mama had been a soft, pretty woman—

Her fingers automatically went to her throat to toy with the locket that was no longer there.

She pressed her hands back into her lap. "Except that I do have my father's nose. I imagine that was the only way my Uncle Richard recognized me when I appeared on his doorstep." Alyss clamped her mouth shut, knowing she'd said too much.

Sinclair's arm was stretched along the side of the settee. He hadn't retreated as far from her as she'd originally thought. The edge of his finger toyed with the bit of blanket over her shoulder.

"I never had my father's nose." Sinclair chuckled and touched the bridge of his. "And even if I did, I wouldn't any longer. Before you ask, two different fistfights. Same opponent. I am to blame for both."

"I suppose, by your logic, I cannot be a changeling." What a blessing to not be the daughter of Nolan Brooks. It had taken years for Alyss to forgive him and her mother, though Mama's only crime had been in loving Papa to the exclusion of everything else. Even her own life.

She nearly reached for the locket again before remembering it was gone.

The feel of his forefinger, rough and warm, tracing lightly around the base of her throat, had the blood thundering in her ears before he pulled away once more.

"He took the locket, didn't he? The gig driver?"

Alyss told herself to breathe even as her body hummed beneath the blanket. "It wasn't valuable," she stammered. "He won't get much for it."

"I disagree. I think the locket had great value to you, Miss Brooks. And I am sorry for its loss." His fingers slid over the blanket near her feet.

Sinclair was so *unbearably* male. It was rare—as in never—that Alyss found herself feeling dominated by a man. Her own personality was so forthright. So commanding and capable, that the opposite sex rarely approached her. Certainly, one had never been drawn to her or dared to trace a line around her neck. Purposefully. Alyss had ensured she would never find affection or be offered marriage.

She would not end up like Mama.

The collar of Sinclair's shirt was unbuttoned, something she hadn't noticed earlier, exposing the hollow of his throat. A tiny, tempting triangle of skin Alyss couldn't seem to pull her gaze away from. A glimpse of dark hair disappeared into his shirt. Probably covering the sculpted terrain of his chest.

Alyss blinked, struggling to remind herself that Sinclair was not some gentlemanly suitor who had asked to call upon her. No man ever had, save Mr. Clinton. Nor was he a man with whom she had an understanding of some sort. She didn't have one of those either, but thought at some point in her future she might. Alyss had no intention of marrying or falling in love, but that didn't rule out things of a physical nature. Because she might *enjoy* things of a physical nature.

Her eyes stuck on that triangle of skin once more.

What is wrong with me?

He'd kidnapped her only this morning and here she was cooing over him like some schoolgirl. Perhaps that was part of his plan. He had been in league with Buckmore. He might still be.

She drew back. Slapped at his fingers teasing along the blanket.

"Your seductive manner will not work on me. Vile, criminal, kidnapper."

A bemused look struck his face. "You've quite a vocabulary, Miss Brooks. I thought brandy and feeding you would be nefarious enough. Seems I'm wrong."

"I will not be a willing party to your scheme. Horrid mongrel." Alyss lifted her chin.

"I assure you, Miss Brooks. I am not a mongrel born on the wrong side of the blanket. My parents were quite happy in their marriage. Now, as to the rest, I've no idea what you're talking about. I didn't lure you to the cottage. I've plied you with one brandy." He looked at the plate on her lap. "And some chicken. What scheme have I concocted?"

"My uncle will not negotiate with you," she snapped, shrinking back as he slid across the settee in her direction. "No matter what your demands. You'll see not one pound." She stared him down, resolved to show no fear, bristling with the rightness of her words. "Feel free to keep me here. Tie me, if you must, but—"

"*Keep* you. *Tie* you up? Why Miss Brooks, how bold you are in your seduction," he interrupted, a wicked look glinting in his eye. "Ask nicely and perhaps I will."

A gasp left her sputtering, words unable to form properly. Her mind wasn't working, far too occupied with imagining herself bound, perhaps to the bed and Sinclair hovering over her. Dear God, her nipples were hardening at the thought, pebbling into painful buds.

Alyss, get ahold of yourself.

"What a vulgar suggestion," she retorted.

Sinclair raised one brow.

"What I meant," Alyss stated firmly, "was that any attempts to ransom me would be met with failure. If your hope is to force me to lower my guard so that you can truly abduct me and recoup the sum Buckmore refused to pay you, well you, sir, are sadly mistaken."

"I'm more concerned that you want me to tie you up, Miss Brooks."

"I said no such thing." An unexpected heaviness took up residence between her thighs. One that pulsed gently, sending a ripple through her lower body. Arousal at the thought of being kept a prisoner. By Sinclair.

Good grief.

No more brandy.

She set down the glass.

"I hadn't considered ransom. It isn't something I normally do," he replied. "A distinct possibility. But do you know what I *really* want, Miss Brooks?" Sinclair's voice became a seductive purr that stroked her beneath the blanket.

"I've no idea," she murmured, nearly struck witless by the sound of him and his body leaning so close to hers. As if he might kiss her.

Another gentle pulsing surged up her body.

Alyss had been kissed before. Once. Mr. Clinton had bestowed a tiny peck upon her lips before she danced out of reach of him and his enormous mustache. Afterward, she had declined to allow him to call on her again.

Should she close her eyes?

"I'm wondering if there is a possibility—" Lust transformed Sinclair's features.

"Yes." Her lashes fell to brush her cheeks as she waited.

"I can wrest that chicken leg from you."

Alyss's eyes popped open, to see him nodding towards the plate still in her lap. Thunder boomed, shaking away her ridiculous thoughts of only a moment ago.

Sinclair's lust wasn't for *her*. But the chicken leg.

Alyss had been reduced to a quivering mound of aspic because he wanted her leftovers.

Mortified, she pushed the plate to him. "Be my guest."

"Thank you." Sinclair bit into the leg, white teeth flashing as he made sighs of ecstasy over that stupid piece of chicken. She noted he didn't deny wanting to hold her for ransom.

"Something amiss, Miss Brooks?" He leaned back, smacking his lips, his enjoyment of the chicken leg painfully obvious.

Horrid wretch.

He might annoy her to death before he had a chance to ransom her.

"Nothing at all. Enjoy your chicken."

What sort of man eats a leg of chicken while looking so magnificent? She might faint if he chewed on a slice of apple. Or buttered a slice of bread. The blanket had slid down to expose her shoulder with the neatly tied ribbon. She tugged at the wool, but it was stuck beneath Sinclair.

He grinned at her.

Alyss's insides twisted about pleasantly once more. He had the same allure she thought a highwayman might. Or a pirate. Dangerous to your purse and virtue.

She knew the particulars of physical relations; she'd grown up in a cluster of tents among the tribes her father traveled with. There had been little privacy. Also, Alyss did enjoy a good book and not everything on the shelf in her room could be considered quality literature. She had thought at one point, she might take a lover. A widower, perhaps. There wasn't any need to deny herself a physical relationship, only a romantic one. Her virtue wasn't precious to her or anyone else. More an inconvenience.

Alyss's gaze flicked to Sinclair again. He had the look of a man who knew exactly how to relieve such a burden from her.

The events of the day may have driven me mad.

Why else would she even consider such a thing?

"I should check my clothing," she said inclining her chin in the direction of her dress and underthings.

"Not dry. Still dripping." He stated. "It's only been an hour or so, Miss Brooks. The storm doesn't appear to be lessening anytime soon. It will be a long afternoon and even a longer night. At least you are dry. Warm. Not hungry." He tossed what was left of the chicken leg into the fire. "Don't be distressed. Is this about the chicken? Clearly, *you* didn't want the chicken, little fairy."

"I don't care about the chicken. And stop calling me that." Alyss drew in a breath. "Were I a lesser woman, today's events would have left me sobbing. Or fainting."

"You don't strike me as a fainter, Miss Brooks. I am glad to hear you aren't concerned with the chicken, because I have eaten most of it. Kidnapping leaves one hungry. But Buckmore, though a complete nitwit, left us a good amount of food. There's a wheel of cheese and bread. We can toast it later over the fire. And since you don't care for brandy overmuch, we'll have the wine." He threw her a wink.

Alyss pursed her lips and looked down at the lone bit of apple left on the plate and considered throwing it at him. Sinclair was rather charming in a rough sort of way. And whimsical. He knew about fairies and jinn. Obviously intelligent, despite assuming she was Elizabeth, in addition to his other, more menacing assets. Appealing to Alyss in the most unexpected ways.

"Fine, Mr. Sinclair." She took up the slice of apple. "Since there isn't any more chicken, can I have a bit more apple?"

Chapter Eleven

S HE'D BEEN CONSIDERING throwing the plate at him.
Women generally didn't find Malcolm to be so annoying, but Miss Brooks certainly did. Nor was he usually so chatty, but he liked talking to her. Had she thrown the plate, or attempted it, Malcolm would have had the perfect excuse to wrestle it from her fingers, which would mean touching Miss Brooks. The blanket would slide off. He'd see what that silly little ribbon was meant to hold up.

A slow rumble echoed in his chest.

Every time the blanket she had clasped around her shifted, Malcolm caught tantalizing glimpses of her pale, moonlit flesh. Her toes kept pushing into his thigh as she struggled not to get too close. The chicken leg had been only a means to keep his mind off *her* legs.

And he was still hungry.

He had considered kissing her. Miss Brooks clearly wanted him to; she'd even closed her eyes. That luscious mouth was only inches from his, but Malcolm decided against it. The woman was hell-bent on reporting him to the authorities. And he had some honor left in his miserable soul. Had he truly been a criminal, he would have already tossed Miss Brooks on the bed.

Dear God, he wanted to. If any woman needed a good tupping, it was Alyss Brooks.

Malcolm drummed his fingers.

Earlier, with Buckmore, she'd lost the control with which she spoke and conducted herself. Malcolm wanted her to snap like that with him, preferably as he was notched between her legs.

Miss Brooks, as if reading his thoughts, frowned and shifted again, trying desperately to keep her toes from touching Malcolm's thigh. She reached for the comb sitting on the table.

The blanket slipped. The ribbon came back into view, along with her collarbone.

Malcolm bit the inside of his mouth to stop from groaning.

She avoided his gaze and started to work the comb through the snarl of her hair, which was starting to dry in white-blonde wisps at her temples. A tiny bit of mud fell on the blanket as she worked on a knot. Then a pebble.

Just thinking of those pale, silvery strands trailing over his chest and thighs, or clasped in his fist as he took her roughly, had his cock straining against his trousers. Her heels digging into his back while he—

"Let me help," Malcolm offered, holding out one hand.

The comb paused. Eyes, too large for her face, widened further. "No. Highly improper."

"The blanket is falling off and you can't reach the back. I have sisters, Miss Brooks. I'll have no trouble pretending you're one of them," he lied. "Turn around."

She stared at him a moment longer, but surprisingly, Miss Brooks twisted to give him her back, careful to keep the blanket close, and handed him the comb.

Her hair would be glorious when it was dry and free of snarls. There was a hint of curl in the nearly white strands. He drew his thumb along one lock, delighted when it curled around his thumb.

Miss Brooks cleared her throat.

Gently, Malcolm started to work through the knots in her hair, careful not to tug too hard and cause her pain. She no longer smelled of lilacs, only rain with a touch of mud, but that didn't deter his desire for her in the least. Was Miss Brooks still a virgin?

Malcolm thought the notion highly unlikely, given her age. But she was a lady no matter that she'd been raised in a tent. He didn't have a great deal of experience with well-bred ladies. Malcolm's tastes leaned more towards working class women. Strong, capable women. Not ones that attended balls and charity teas.

He struggled with a difficult snarl, trying to be gentle, resisting the urge to nibble along the slope of her neck. Or lick the curve of her ear. If Malcolm took such a liberty, it might compel her to slap or kick him. He might have to wrestle for control of the blanket.

God, I hope so.

The lower half of Malcolm's body tightened at the thought of subduing Miss Brooks. Perhaps she would disparage him in that delicious crisp, tart accent. Or give him directions on how best to use his mouth and hands on her.

Malcolm shut his eyes, his fingers pausing on the comb.

"Are you finished?" she asked. The entire time he worked on her hair, Miss Brooks hadn't spoken. She'd sat completely still, shoulders tense, careful not to lean back against him.

"I think I've gotten the worst of it."

"Good, now please, remove yourself from the settee."

Probably for the best.

Taking a slow, deep breath, which didn't stop the twitching of his cock in the least, Malcolm stood and went to the small bookshelf set into the wall. Reading might help take his mind off of her and all the things Malcolm considered doing.

The titles and subjects of the tomes were so varied, he suspected Buckmore had just walked into a bookseller's and asked for a selection of books that might look impressive sitting on a shelf.

His fingers stopped at a book on animal husbandry bound in green leather. Cracking it open, the smell of paper and ink greeted him. Malcolm chuckled. He'd been correct.

The book had never been opened.

Not surprising. Another book was Roman military history. Ancient Greeks. Native plants of England. Barely acquainted with Buckmore and even Malcolm knew the titled twit hadn't read any of these.

"Anything of interest?" Miss Brooks sounded hopeful.

"Animal husbandry. Greek history. Roman battles. Oh, and this," Malcolm held up a slim book. *"Don Juan* by Byron."

"One of Buckmore's female companions must have left that." She wiggled her fingers. "I'll take it, please."

A soft sheen of pink covered her cheeks at the light brush of his fingertips along her own as he handed her the book. "Are you certain you don't want to learn the various aspects of sheep breeding?" he asked.

The color in her cheeks deepened. "No, thank you."

Malcolm peered further into the shelf, catching sight of one last book, smaller than the others, stuck in the back. He pulled it out with a smile. Shakespeare. And in a fantastic bit of coincidence, the volume contained *A Midsummer Night's Dream.*

There hadn't been much to read at Dunnings, but Malcolm's mother did have the collected works of William Shakespeare which consisted of several volumes. It was one of her most treasured possessions. She always traveled with Shakespeare so when the entire family arrived in London at the death of Malcolm's father, the book was in her trunks. Had Lady Longwood or Bentley discovered her collection, they would have taken Shakespeare out of spite if nothing else.

Mother read to Malcolm and his siblings nearly every night at Dunnings from those slender volumes, changing her voice for every character, pacing about the room with great drama.

Until she became too sick to do so.

His fingers tightened on the book.

A memory flashed before him, of the shabby drawing room at Dunnings. Mother pausing to cough blood into a handkerchief as she acted out the parts of one of the plays she had so adored. Bentley had gotten off easy having his neck snapped in a carriage accident. Malcolm's plans for his demise would have been far more painful.

"An interesting choice," Miss Brooks said coolly. "I hadn't thought a mercenary would enjoy Shakespeare."

"I've never said I was a mercenary, Miss Brooks. Though you keep insisting." He pushed the memory of Dunnings away. "My mother adored Shakespeare. She was an actress."

"An actress?"

Malcolm cursed silently at having let his guard down. He'd been caught up in a momentary lapse of grief, thinking of his mother, and he'd slipped. Sinclair was a common enough name, but being a Sinclair *and* having a mother who trod the stage made you a *Deadly Sin*. And though he hadn't mentioned Tamsin by name, her ability to punch better than any prizefighter would provide another clue.

Sooner or later, Miss Brooks might put the pieces of his identity together.

He really should just walk out into the storm, find someplace else to spend the night and leave for London at first light. Miss Brooks wouldn't have any trouble surviving on her own. In fact, she might prefer it.

Instead, Malcolm deliberately ignored the chair before the fire, and sat once more on the edge of the settee, smiling as Miss Brooks squeaked in protest. Nothing could force him out of this cottage, not even the threat of imprisonment at her hands. He was far too intrigued by her—a rarity when it came to women—for him to leave her.

The stupid bow at her shoulder taunted him, begging Malcolm to just pull the ribbon loose.

Untold delights existed if he pulled it free. Maybe with his teeth.

"Is there any tea?" she inquired, paging through the book. "I need something to warm me other than brandy." Miss Brooks scowled at the tiny bit of brandy left in her glass as if it had personally insulted her.

Malcolm knew of something that would warm her quicker than tea or brandy. Him. But he dutifully came to his feet, careful to keep the lower half of his body turned away from Miss Brooks, though she was already buried in the book.

"Let me find a kettle."

CHAPTER TWELVE

A LYSS SHUT THE book in her lap. Byron had a tendency to make her temples ache. She'd had quite enough of his romantic tripe. Roman military history would have been much more absorbing but she hadn't asked for that book because Sinclair had offered it.

Glancing out the window, a sigh of resignation left her at the rain pouring with such intensity from the sky. The storm had not lessened a bit as night began to fall, the gloom of the surrounding woods circling the sanctuary of the cottage. She snuggled further into the blanket, hearing the hiss of moisture come down the chimney.

Her abductor seemed engrossed in his book of Shakespeare, not once looking in her direction since fetching her a pot of tea. Sinclair had not come back to the settee and instead, settled himself in one of the chairs by the fire.

She was oddly disappointed. And her toes were cold without his bulk warming his end of the settee. Alyss reached for another biscuit. Sinclair had found a tin along with a small pot of honey and brought it with the tea. Considering he'd eaten all the chicken; Alyss didn't bother to share the biscuits.

The silence between them wasn't uncomfortable, considering their relationship. Had he reconsidered holding her for ransom and hadn't yet told Alyss? She should be afraid for her safety. Afraid of him. Yet she wasn't.

This was by far the strangest, most absurd thing that had ever happened to her, and she'd been raised in the desert.

She placed Lord Byron on the table beside her. "You said you had sisters."

Sinclair didn't look up or answer immediately. He deliberately finished the page he was reading before answering. "You should be less obvious at your attempts to gain more information about me to pass to the authorities, Miss Brooks. I'd hoped the biscuits would have helped. Or the honey. Neither sweetened you up."

Alyss gave a tiny snort. "Only toffee cake has such a power."

The sides of his mustache twitched. "Pity, we've no toffee cake. But if there were any in the cottage, I would have already eaten it. One more detail to add to your list. I love toffee cake."

"I'm sure the information will be crucial to apprehending you. I can send Bow Street runners to every bakery in London."

"Never said that's where I was going, Miss Brooks."

Alyss hid a smile. She liked the sound of him. That odd combination of patrician accent mixed with the rolling of Northumberland. "It was an educated guess, Mr. Sinclair. Besides, I'm bored with Byron. I don't suppose you found a deck of cards or a chessboard while poking about?"

He shut his own book. "I have two sisters, Miss Brooks. Two brothers. One older. You should be taking notes."

"And the other brother?" The longer Alyss spent in his company, letting him make her tea and bring her biscuits, the less inclination she had to report him to the authorities. She wasn't about to let him know that, of course.

Sinclair stayed quiet for so long, Alyss thought perhaps his brother had died. She was about to apologize for asking when he said, "My twin." He frowned as if admitting to a twin was exceptionally painful.

"You have a twin brother? But you said before that—"

"We aren't identical. You wouldn't even know we were related if you saw us together. As different as night and day. And before you ask, he doesn't share my hobby of kidnapping spinsters."

Alyss tapped her chin. Sinclair was much more amusing than Byron. "Butcher? Sailor? Farmer?"

There was no change in his expression, no tell that any of her guesses had been correct.

"Solicitor. Or a ratcatcher."

A small bark of laughter came from him. "Dear god, he had one fall in his porridge once. So, no."

That was certainly interesting, but not helpful. "Gambler."

The light shifted in Sinclair's eyes, the only sign she was close to the truth.

"I suppose that is a *sort* of mercenary, a gambler," she pressed. "A man who makes his living at cards. Or is it dice? I've heard of hazard." Alyss paused. "In the desert, there was a game the men played with the bones of a bird."

"In hazard, the odds always favor the house. Difficult to make a living when you must rely on pure luck and no skill. Especially if one is using bird bones. What kind of bird?"

"I don't know. A vulture of some sort. A devil bird."

Sinclair's eyes never strayed from hers. "You are endlessly surprising."

Alyss's heart made an odd sort of flutter, something that kept happening since she'd been thrown over his broad shoulders in the park. That seemed a lifetime ago even though it had only been this morning.

"So, your brother is a card player," Alyss said. "As disreputable as you."

"He isn't in the least. Women adore him. You'd find him charming. Detests cabbage, the country, and farm animals. Pigs in particular." A small laugh came from him.

"I'm not fond of cabbage either," Alyss offered. "You miss him."

"Greatly. What sort of antiquities did your father collect in the desert?"

The instant he said the words, the grit of sand filled her mouth. The smell of the camels that had carried their packs. Unwashed bodies around a central fire. "Mr. Nolan Brooks would have told you he was a scholar. He fancied himself an academic. But in reality, my father was something of a treasure hunter. He wasn't very good at it." Alyss tried to hide the bitterness that bled into her words and failed.

"You become more interesting by the moment, Miss Brooks."

Her heart squeezed at his words. She had been called many things in her life, but no one ever said Alyss was interesting.

"The desert is barren. Dry. Dirty. I don't miss it. He insisted we must all exist in a sand-filled tent, traveling with various tribes or other nomads as he searched about for an idol or a hidden temple. Gold. Jewels." Alyss lifted a hand. "He made observations in small notebooks no one would ever bother to read." Papa hadn't been well thought of in academic circles. At times, she wondered what had happened to the dozens of notebooks Papa had once written in, but she supposed they were lost to the desert.

As her mother had been.

Alyss could still smell the blood. The scent of something dying. The mound of blankets Mama had been buried under.

"And what about your mother, Miss Brooks? Did she care for the desert?"

"She cared for my father mostly."

Mama begged to go back to London. Pleaded. She was with child and didn't want to give birth in the desert with only a filthy old woman and Alyss to help her. But in the end, Nolan Brooks refused to leave the desert and Mama couldn't bear to leave him. Her love for him came at a steep cost. Her life.

Alyss had held her dead mother's hand until someone finally found Nolan Brooks. She'd screamed her grief and hatred at him. Demanded he send her to London. Her course was set after that.

Sinclair studied her intently before saying, "I couldn't save my mother either." He stood and marched to the back of the cottage.

"I'll fetch us something to eat."

Alyss fell back against the settee, wondering that a man she barely knew had seen inside her so easily. No one else had. Not even Uncle Richard. She pressed her fingers into the blanket listening to Sinclair moving about, preparing their food. He was exposing her in small layers. Trying to force Alyss to let down her guard. Cede control. Making her bloody tea. Giving her biscuits. Reading with her. Now she was allowing it again.

Sinclair returned with a tray of sliced cheese, bread, and butter. A bottle of wine was clasped in his free hand. He placed everything on the low table in front of the settee before cursing under his breath. Returning to the other side of the cottage once more, he then reappeared with two glasses.

"Don't think for an instant that this"—she waved her hand between them—"comradery, means *anything*. Knowing more about each other will not make me sympathetic. Don't befriend me. It won't stop me," she said, though less forcefully than before. "From—

"Do you want wine or not, Miss Brooks?"

DEFIANT LITTLE FAIRY.

Her mother had died in that desert and Malcolm would bet that she'd witnessed it. The bitterness towards her father, the blame she placed on him was evident in every line of her body.

The urge to comfort her. Protect her. Had overwhelmed him. He'd had to force himself to walk away. He would make them both something to eat. They'd share the wine. He'd engage her in conversation that didn't immediately have them baring their souls to each other. Then he'd point her in the direction of the bed on the other side of the cottage and tamp down his unbridled desire for this troublesome woman. He'd return her to London tomorrow morning. There was a coaching inn they'd passed on the way to Gerryhill, just on the outskirts of town. He could easily find her a hack from there.

Until then, Malcolm meant to keep his distance.

She shifted on the settee, eyes deep fathomless pools of near ebony, far too large for her delicate face, watching him. The blanket had completely fallen from her shoulders, and she was so irritated she'd failed to notice. That swathe of pale skin topped by that stupid bow had Malcolm's fingers twitching with the urge to touch her.

It was bound to be a long night.

Efficiently, Malcolm sliced up the bread, slathered it with some butter, and put the cheese between the two halves. Carefully, using a pair of tongs, he lifted it near the flames to toast each side and melt the cheese.

A puff of annoyance came from the settee. "You're going to burn it."

A shiver went up Malcolm's spine at the authoritative tone. If Miss Brooks had any idea how close he was to tossing her on the rug beneath his feet and tearing away the blanket, she might not have opened her mouth.

"I am not burning it." He turned back to the flames and lifted the bread a little higher. The edge *was* slightly burned, but that didn't bother Malcolm.

The sound of her sliding off the settee, and the blanket swishing about, met his ears.

Malcolm refused to turn.

"I don't care for blackened toast and cheese. Let me do it."

Her hair was nearly dry, so white-blonde she nearly glowed in the darkened confines of the cottage. Lightning streaked across the sky outside, visible through the window behind her. Malcolm's heart stuttered at the sheer beauty of Miss Alyss Brooks. But that didn't stop him from jerking the tongs back in his direction and out of her reach.

"I know what I'm doing. I've cooked over a fire dozens of times." He bit his tongue.

"So have I." Alyss snorted. "Give me that." She came to her knees, so intent on wresting the tongs from his grasp, she failed to notice the blanket had slipped to her waist. "I'm hungry and don't desire burned toast and cheese. Thanks to you, there's little else."

"You devoured a bloody tin of biscuits," he growled back. "I was never even offered one." Malcolm inhaled Alyss's scent mixed with the rainwater. Warm woman and the wool of the blanket. Honestly, he didn't care about the bloody toasted bread and cheese. Or the wine. Not with the sight of her nipples straining against the sheer material of whatever she was wearing. He could see the glorious outline of her breasts.

Jesus.

An acrid smell hit his nose. Something was burning and it wasn't the bread. She had leaned too close to the fire and a spark had fallen on the blanket.

"The blanket," he growled, letting go of the tongs to slap at the blanket. "Are you trying to set yourself ablaze? Is it that important to instruct me on toasting bread and cheese?"

"You obviously have no skill at it," she snapped, her body arching in his direction.

The gentle bounce of her breasts. Her nipples were peaked. Hard. And he could see them clearly.

Malcolm had shown a great deal of restraint up until now.

The tongs fell into the fire just as his lips made contact with the slope of her neck. He pressed a greedy kiss to the silk of her skin. The resolution of moments ago to leave her untouched faded as the attraction between them finally erupted.

"Oh," she gasped.

Encouraged that Miss Brooks didn't immediately try to impale him with the poker, Malcolm licked at the side of her neck, taking small nibbles, as if he were eating his way around the edges of a cake. A delicious, tart, possibly sour, cake that Malcolm had to have, no matter the cost.

A low, sensuous moan came from her, as if the last vestiges of her control were snapping.

"Just because we've shared a secret or two doesn't give you leave to take liberties. And you've ruined the toast."

"Do you want me to stop?" he murmured just beneath her ear. "Now would be the time. Soldiers, once engaged in their objective, rarely retreat."

"I knew you were once a soldier." Slender fingers curled into Malcolm's shirt, tugging at the frayed linen as if she wished to curl herself into his chest. "And only cowards retreat, Mr. Sinclair."

CHAPTER THIRTEEN

ALYSS'S MIND WAS set the moment she was greeted with his muscular backside as he toasted the bread before the fire. She was thirty. Still a virgin. Frankly, she didn't want to wait for some silver-haired widower to take her virtue and possibly be compelled to offer marriage. She wanted to give it to Sinclair. Former soldier. Likely a mercenary. Not a criminal only a man *capable* of criminal acts.

And he'd made her tea.

After tomorrow, Alyss would never see him again. There would be no conversation of a future. No talk of marriage. There was no danger of falling in love. They hardly knew each other.

She might never have such an opportunity again.

This moment felt right, as few others had.

Impulsively, Alyss pressed a tentative, delicate kiss to the hollow of his neck, the place she'd wished to touch with her lips for hours. Her eyes closed at the exquisite taste of him. She licked along that spot, wondering if she was doing things properly when Sinclair's larger body trembled.

"Miss Brooks," it came out in a long sigh.

The voice of reason, the one that kept her tightly restrained, stomped, and screamed that Alyss had put herself in a terribly precarious position. She should stand, take the blanket and retreat to the other side of the cottage, fiercely protecting her virtue.

Alyss ignored the annoying whisper, pushing the voice aside

without another thought.

Sinclair dropped his chin and stared at her mouth. "The things," he whispered. "I want to do to this mouth." The edge of his finger traced along her bottom lip, before brushing his mouth gently over hers.

Alyss's entire body jolted, as much from his lips as his words.

A broad palm, rough even through the thin silk, cupped her breast as his lips once more pressed hers, this time with purpose. His thumb circled the tip of one nipple, pulling at the hardened peak, torturing sensation out of her slowly. His lips grew more insistent. Urgent. A flood of pleasure eased down her body, stroked by his hand and mouth to nestle between her thighs with a pleasurable ache.

Alyss kissed him back, not hesitant, not willing to let him guess at her lack of experience. She had already decided not to admit to her virginity, afraid he might pull away from her. And she wanted this, and him, so much.

Muscle greeted her palms as she placed them on the broad chest, stretching her fingers across the sculpted expanse. She slid her hand inside his shirt, nails grazing along warm skin. His chest was covered with hair that scratched and curled against her fingers.

He pulled back, looking down at her and Alyss wished she could make out the green of his eyes. "Tell me to stop, little fairy."

"No." Alyss shook her head. "I'm no maid," she lied, feeling exceptionally daring. Tracing her thumb along his bottom lip she murmured, "Though admittedly, not terribly experienced."

He nipped at her thumb, then slowly sucked the digit into his mouth.

Such a small thing to make her thighs tremble.

Sinclair released her thumb and his mouth fell on hers with such hunger that Alyss could barely take a breath. His teeth grabbed at her lower lip, tongue sweeping inside her mouth to savor and taste her. He didn't ask for her surrender, he demanded it. The hand in her hair tightened, pulling at the strands while he kissed her, the sting sending another wave of sensation down her body.

He slowly leaned back, taking her with him, until they both lay on the floor.

"Alyss," he whispered against her mouth with so much longing she nearly wept.

Something tugged inside her, pulled at her heart, but she refused to allow it to take root.

His mouth left hers to trail over her neck, the spot beneath her ear, teasing along her collarbone to her shoulder. Teeth tearing into the bow, he ripped the ribbon from her shoulder. The wisp of fabric fluttered away exposing one breast.

"God, you're beautiful. Tell me what you want me to do."

Alyss blinked. She truly hadn't a clue, only more of what he'd been doing.

His tongue flicked out to glide along her nipple.

"Yes, that," she panted softly. "More of that."

Sinclair tore at the rest of the nightgown like some wild animal in his haste to bare her completely. The action should have terrified her; instead, it sent warmth pooling about her body. Teeth grazed her nipple, sucking and licking until her entire melted and writhed beneath his.

He turned her carefully, so that the glow of the fire lit against her skin. Hands caressed her skin, explored every hollow, his mouth tasting her breasts while she arched beneath him. Each nipple was circled with agonizing slowness by his tongue, pulling a cry from her lips. His mouth trailed along the line of her ribs and stomach. The curve of her hips before his palm splayed possessively over her stomach.

"A fairy princess." The low timbre of his voice soothed her. "A fairy princess," he murmured, dipping his mouth to lick around the edge of her hip. "My fairy."

His hand moved between her thighs, tugging gently at the fluff of hair atop her mound. A forefinger dipped lower, sliding through her wetness.

Alyss's hips jerked. No one had ever touched her there. "I—" she bit her tongue, mindful that Sinclair assumed she'd been bedded before. "Am not terribly experienced," she warned him again.

"I'm still hungry."

"You—ate all the chicken and burnt the bread," she stammered stupidly as he shifted to place his broad shoulders between her legs, parting them with one big hand.

"Such beautiful hair." Fingers threaded through the tuft atop her mound, before cupping her sex. Moisture spilled between her thighs as he pushed with the heel of his palm, watching her the entire time.

"Has anyone ever tasted you, Alyss?"

Tasted her? Goodness, no one had ever—

"I'll take that as a no. A travesty. For any man to ignore such a feast." His hand trailed along her thigh, drawing small circles with the tip of one finger. A slow, lazy lick of his tongue along the folds of her flesh followed.

"Oh." The word ended in a low moan of pleasure. Her hands fell to his head, threading through the thick strands of hair.

The flat of his tongue explored, teasing at her folds, stroking lightly over the small bud at the center which swelled and pulsed with each caress. Alyss twisted beneath him, shocked to find her hands forcing his head and mouth more fully against her.

A finger, feeling far larger than it looked, eased inside her while his tongue continued to lick and suck. The finger pressed gently at a spot along her inner wall—

"Bloody hell," she gasped as her pleasure intensified tenfold.

Lifting his head, Sinclair's tongue paused, but the twist of his finger, now joined by a second, continued. "I do love the sound of a curse coming from you, Alyss. But I'll like hearing you beg even more."

"Oh." A moan passed her lips as his tongue flicked along the edges of that tiny nub.

His free hand took hold of her hip, keeping her in place.

Between the torture of his tongue and the insistent stroking of his finger, Alyss's control, what little she had left, shattered. Words came out of her, begging. Commanding. Vulgar, filthy things Alyss would never normally say.

A chuckle came from deep in his chest, vibrating into her skin. "Finally," she heard him whisper. He pushed her up a summit so laden with exquisite bliss that Alyss thought she might die if she didn't reach the top. When she got close, his tongue and fingers paused and she took a shaky breath, still on edge, feeling as if she might break apart if only—

Over and over, he took her up, only to leave Alyss suspended and writhing beneath him. Her body clasped the fingers deep inside her. Panting, her back arched, she snarled at him. "You bloody"—One fist pummeled his shoulder. "Please. I can't—"

Sinclair's hand moved from her hip to her breast, and grabbing at her nipple, he rolled and squeezed, pinching it between his thumb and forefinger. The sting shot straight between Alyss's thighs, to the spot which begged for release. Then his tongue, purposefully, blissfully, sucked that small nub into his mouth, grazing softly with his teeth.

She came apart, her entire body bursting into tiny shards to scatter on the floor before the fire. Dear lord, her vision clouded over, she saw nothing but bits of light as her eyes closed. Limbs and hips jerking, waves of pleasure flowed over every inch of her.

Oh. I'm so pleased I didn't wait for some doddering widower.

It was her last coherent thought as Sinclair wrung every ounce of pleasure from Alyss with his mouth and fingers, until she lay stunned, panting, and naked before him.

Sinclair pressed a kiss to the middle of her stomach, his fingers leaving her body, then once more possessively cupping her sex.

Well, yes, there was no doubt of his ownership of that part of her anatomy.

"Stay as you are. Don't move." He rolled to his side and took the bottle of wine but neglected the glasses. He threw his head back and took several swallows before pausing. "Thirsty work, pleasing you, Alyss Brooks."

Had he asked her at that moment to chain herself to him, Alyss wouldn't have hesitated.

CHAPTER FOURTEEN

MALCOLM WANTED TO sink his teeth into Alyss. Put his hands and mouth on every part of her. Especially his cock. Possessiveness, harsh and sharp, dug in its claws. He'd never experienced such a fierceness for a woman before. One he hadn't even yet properly bedded.

Alyss, his fairy. A sight to behold with the firelight shining on the white-blonde hair as if she were made of moonlight. Even between her legs. Full, rounded breasts topped with delicious pink nipples. Generous hips made for his hands. A tongue which would rip a man to shreds before using it for other, more useful things.

He handed her the bottle of wine, surprised she took a healthy swallow. But Alyss had already lost her control. He'd seen it. Heard it.

"I'm the only one naked, Mr. Sinclair."

That concise, authoritative tone had him sucking in his breath.

Malcolm tugged at his shirt, arms flexing as he tossed the garment over one of the chairs.

Alyss watched him with those impossibly fathomless eyes, taking in his shoulders and chest. "What is that?" she nodded at a perfectly round scar just below his collarbone.

"Pistol." He traced a jagged scar along his ribs. "Sword. I didn't move quick enough."

Her eyes widened, but she didn't comment.

The boots were next, tossing them to the side with a thud before shucking off the trousers and what little he had in the way of underthings. His cock jutted out, thick and hard, pointed directly at Miss Alyss Brooks.

Any inexperienced young lady would blush at the sight of a naked man. In Malcolm's case, given his assets, she might faint. A woman who'd had a lover wouldn't be nearly as shocked.

Alyss just stared, eyes wide and unblinking.

"Alyss." A thought occurred to Malcolm, though he couldn't imagine what purpose it would serve for her to claim she wasn't a maid, if she was. "You *have* done this before?"

"Don't be ridiculous," she snapped. "I'm thirty."

Malcolm wasn't surprised. He'd known she was older than he, but not by how much. Only a few years.

"I am unwed by choice." She took another swallow of the wine and raised a brow, nodding in the direction of his cock. "Impressive for a kidnapper."

"Make sure." Malcolm came to the floor beside her. "To include that in your description of me to the authorities."

BOLD, ALYSS. VERY bold.

She had to say something that would deter him from guessing at her deception. It wasn't as if she was doing anything truly dishonest by withholding the information. They'd never see each other again after this tiny bubble, built from a thunderstorm and Buckmore's cottage, burst. But she had sensed a streak of morality in Sinclair, yet another clue that he wasn't all he appeared to be. And Alyss didn't want him attempting to do something honorable if he knew he'd taken her virtue.

The idea was ridiculous. She was a woman of thirty. An avowed spinster. Unwed by choice.

Alyss decided it more important to concentrate on the splendid beast before her. The muscular, impossibly broad chest with the dusting of dark hair. Flat stomach, with not a hint of overindulgence and the sharp indentation of his hipbones, all culminating in a thatch of dark hair from which protruded a most impressive male appendage. She assumed it would be considered impressive. Alyss had nothing to compare Sinclair to. She'd actually never seen a man's anatomy before. Only that of camels.

Still, Sinclair appeared to be—more endowed than she'd expected. If Alyss were the sort of lady who swooned, now would be the appropriate time considering she was expected to take *that*—inside her.

Mrs. Hitchcock, her uncle's delightful widow friend, had far too much ratafia one night after dinner. She also wrongfully assumed Alyss was entertaining thoughts of Mr. Clinton and sought to help guide her in the absence of any other women. Mrs. Hitchcock had referred to that part of the male anatomy as a gentleman's *length*.

Alyss took in the scene before her.

Length indeed. But Mrs. Hitchcock had made no mention of *circumference*.

"Something worrying you, Miss Brooks?"

"Not at all." She pushed aside her concerns. Sinclair obviously knew what he was doing as evidenced earlier. If Alyss could have more of *that,* she might be able to tolerate that enormous appendage.

His features softened as he came to her, one hand trailing lightly over the curve of her hip. "Things appear daunting. I'll be careful." Sinclair kissed her gently.

Alyss wound her arms around his neck, sinking her fingers into his hair. She didn't even mind all the beard and mustache overly much when he kissed her so softly. As if he cherished her. Such a lovely feeling.

"So will I," she assured him. "Be careful, that is."

"Oh, Miss Brooks," he chuckled, and came down on all fours, looming over her, savagely magnificent and entirely male with lines of sculpted muscle across his arms and thighs.

Alyss decided to memorize everything about Sinclair. Not to give to the authorities, but so that she would recall these moments with him in the future and relieve them. Something to warm Alyss when she was no more than Elizabeth's elderly relation, relegated to the corner of the drawing room.

Their mouths found each other, possessive and insistent, because Alyss thought of Sinclair as hers, even if for only one night. Cedar clung to his skin, along with leather and horse. He tasted of wine and something musky that she belatedly realized was her. Featherlight touches skimmed over her breasts, caressing Alyss until the blood beneath her skin once more warmed and that delicious ache returned between her thighs.

He stroked her throat, before stretching his fingers through the tangles of her hair. Wedging himself more fully between her thighs, Alyss felt the hot press of him at her entrance and tensed.

Would it hurt? It was her understanding it did, the first time. Another tidbit Mrs. Hitchcock shared with her, but she'd also said that not every woman was the same. Alyss might only feel a pinch. Or nothing at all.

Alyss kissed him harder. Her fingers moved down his shoulders and back, stretching over the muscles, scratching his skin with her nails. Part of her wanted to confess the truth to him, but no purpose would be served in him knowing. She had no expectations of him beyond tonight. He might well be gone when she awoke in the morning.

Sinclair thrust inside her in one stroke, shocking Alyss and forcing her hips to rock back, taking him deeper. Her breath caught and held, her body unable to think beyond the painful stretching sensation and the tiny pinch heralding the loss of her maidenhead. He was overly large. Why else would Alyss feel as if she was nearly torn asunder? She bit back a whimper, inner muscles fluttering like the wings of a butterfly around the hardness invading her.

Alyss didn't dare let him know.

So, she hid her discomfort by sinking her teeth into his chest.

CHAPTER FIFTEEN

MALCOLM TRIED TO be gentle. He did. He was a fairly big man, heavy. His cock was no exception. He'd felt her body's resistance though he'd prepared her as best he could. But her body was clamped tightly around his, so much so, Malcom felt lightheaded.

But then Alyss bit him, small teeth tearing at his skin. Something a vicious fairy or an overly stern governess might do to make a point. The little control Malcolm still possessed, snapped. He took her roughly, like some bloody savage. The need to imprint himself on the slender, moonlit body overriding all common sense.

His hand grasped her hip, fingers sinking into the softness of her buttocks. His teeth grazed along the pristine white of her shoulder, leaving a mark to match the one she'd given him.

A cry left her. Pain and pleasure mixed together. "Yes."

Malcolm withdrew slowly before thrusting once more, so hard her delicate form slid across the rug. He wanted to devour her.

Alyss lifted her hips up, purring against him like some wild cat. She clawed at him, urging Malcolm deeper with each thrust.

Dear God, the sounds that came from her.

There was a desperation to their joining, a violent battle of wills, each unable to relinquish control to the other. Restraint, what little either of them possessed, had long since fled.

"Alyss," he growled next to her ear, sucking in the lobe, and drawing his teeth over the edge.

He kept his fingers tangled in her hair, pulling at the moonlit strands, bending her body to his will. Slowing his movements, he twisted his hips, catching at the place they were joined.

A low moan came from her lips. "More, vile kidnapper."

A smile flitted on his lips.

Pressing their foreheads together, Malcolm held her down, staring into the abyss of her eyes as he took her, marveling at every emotion on her face. Inhaling each breath, listening to the soft, feminine sounds of pleasure. Her body tightened around his, signaling her impending release and bringing about his own. Pulling it from Malcolm as Alyss demanded his surrender.

Her name, broken and ragged, left him, the sound of his climax echoing in the room, singeing every nerve of his body until his skin felt blistered from the intensity. Malcolm struggled to catch his breath, panting for air even as his chin lowered to nuzzle against Alyss's neck.

Dear lord. The entire world seemed to have shifted for Malcolm.

They lay together before the fire, skin damp with sweat, the only sounds the rain beating against the windows.

"If your intent is to suffocate me, you are succeeding," she murmured, her fingers stroking lightly down his cheek. "I think it is the overabundance of facial hair."

Malcolm rolled to the side. Tiny marks decorated her shoulders and breasts where he'd nipped and sucked, red and stark against the pale white of her skin. "I'm a beast," he whispered, pressing a kiss of apology along the side of one breast. He had never behaved with so little restraint. But that need to fuse himself to Alyss had been overwhelming. And still it hummed inside him, demanding Malcolm take her again.

"A magnificent beast." Alyss curled into his chest. "I'm perfectly well. Better than I have ever been."

Malcolm could fall to his death inside the fathomless pitch of her eyes. Gladly. His lips trailed along Alyss's temple, breathing her in. "I do not regret mistaking you for your cousin, Alyss Brooks. Or the matter of your abduction at all."

CHAPTER SIXTEEN

ALYSS AWOKE WARM and content, snuggling further into the blanket, even as sunlight pricked against the lids of her eyes. She hadn't slept so soundly in years and had no desire to leave the nest of blankets surrounding her. The only thing ruining her absolute enjoyment of the soft mattress at her back was an annoying, insistent poking in the area of her ribcage.

"Alyss. Get up." A growl sounded.

She shook her head and rolled over. "Go away."

Another poke.

Her eyes blinked open to see an unfamiliar wall painted in cream with a tiny crack at the corner. The screen she'd changed behind last night was before her, along with the armoire, still open with an assortment of lacy garments spilling out.

Buckmore's cottage. Alyss rolled over.

Sinclair hovered over the bed, fully dressed, munching on a bit of cheese, behaving as if he'd just come upon her walking in the park.

"The rain has stopped. You must get up." He gave her a friendly glance, took another bite of cheese and moved away. His manner gave no indication of the intimacies they'd shared from the previous night—*good grief.*

A blush bloomed across her cheeks.

So many intimacies.

The soreness between her thighs, as well as her nakedness

beneath the blankets informed Alyss that not one bit of that had been a dream. All real. She'd been bedded by the man who'd abducted her.

Sinclair stomping about the bed, rather impatiently. "I made you tea," he said, over his shoulder. "Most of the bread is burned. But there's an apple or two and some cheese. There is also some eggs, but I don't think it wise to linger."

Alyss's romantic interlude was at an end. Not that she'd had any expectations of the passion from last night to survive in the cold light of day. That had rather been the point.

She didn't recall being carried to bed last night, but she hadn't been in a position to think too much. Her mind had gone blank sometime during Sinclair's third tupping of her body which now felt as if it were made of warm taffy. That last time Alyss had been on her knees, fingers curled around the cushions of the chair while he thrust into her from behind, her hair twisted around his wrist. Alyss had screamed out her release, sobbing into the chair at being ravaged to within an inch of her life.

Good lord.

The woman last night had behaved with a great deal of indecency and could not possibly have been Alyss Brooks.

She sat up, glancing at the pillow beside her noting the slight indentation. He'd slept beside her last night. Alyss's heart constricted for some ridiculous reason.

"Splendid," she said with as much enthusiasm as she could muster. Shifting to the side of the bed, she winced again at the ache between her thighs. She felt bruised. Slightly battered. And absolutely marvelous.

Alyss regretted *nothing*.

Sinclair tossed another bit of cheese into the air and caught it in his mouth. "The storm ended sometime after midnight." He chewed. "The roads should be passable. There shouldn't be any problem getting you back to London, Miss Brooks. We can leave as soon as you're ready," his voice was gruff but polite.

Alyss composed her features into politeness as well, hating

that he'd so easily reverted back into a stranger, though it was certainly for the best. She only hadn't expected that the loss of intimacy between them would be so abrupt. But what had she expected? Breakfast in bed. Shared laughter. Perhaps they'd just set up house in Buckmore's cottage and spend the day skipping through the fields picking wildflowers.

Ridiculous.

"It isn't necessary to return me to London," the words came out precise and sharp. "I can manage on my own."

"Clearly, you cannot, Miss Brooks. Buckmore may have instructed the entire hamlet to leave you to wander about. I left your things over there," Sinclair gestured to her dress and petticoats beside the screen. "Still a bit muddy, but no longer wet."

The dress, one of her favorites, looked as if someone had beaten the fabric with rocks. But the dried mud could be brushed off, she supposed. Enough to appear presentable. "How do you propose a trip to London be accomplished? I think it as unlikely as I in finding a carriage willing to take us back. If London is your destination."

Sinclair had never actually said where he intended to go.

"I've taken care of arrangements," he assured her in a friendly tone. "Hurry up."

Rather anxious to be rid of her, wasn't he? Alyss had thought he would at least—

Urge her to run away with him to parts unknown? Ask permission to call upon her? He wasn't a gentleman, even if it seemed likely he'd begun life as one. She didn't even know his given name. It wasn't as if they'd been properly introduced at a dinner party or ball. Last night had been—an aberration of sorts. A moment in time that would not come again.

An oily sensation spilled into her mid-section.

Or *perhaps* last night had been Sinclair's way of ensuring Alyss didn't go to the authorities. Worse, he could still be in league with Buckmore. He had disappeared in the direction of the stables shortly before Alyss ventured there herself and hadn't seemed at all surprised to see her last night.

Had her seduction been on Buckmore's orders? Or did Sinclair have another purpose?

Alyss had been deliberately stranded at Gerryhill, after all. Unable to return to her uncle's home with news of Buckmore. She'd spent the night with a complete stranger. Even though everyone in London considered her a spinster, firmly on the shelf, but there would still be repercussions for her reputation, Buckmore's doing or not.

"I'll leave you to get dressed, Miss Brooks. I'll douse the fire after you're finished." Sinclair stepped out of the cottage to give her privacy.

She stood on shaking legs and went to take up her ruined clothing, trying not to look at the proof of what she'd done. Tiny bite marks along her stomach. The skin of her inner thighs was chafed from Sinclair's beard. And finally, barely noticeable, one lone speck of dried blood. The only visible proof she'd lost her virtue.

Her fingers trembled as she slipped the dress over her head. The fit was tight, but her corset was beyond repair. She picked up the destroyed garment, strolled over to the fireplace and tossed it in.

Sinclair had tidied the cottage while she slept, removing the plates, and burnt toast from the night before. The wine was gone. The books put back on the shelf. Alyss stared at the rug before the fire, thinking of what had occurred there last night.

It was entirely possible that her ruination had been less about physical desire and more a way to keep Alyss Brooks silent.

What an ugly, unwelcome thought.

She struggled a bit with the buttons on the back of her dress, but refused to call Sinclair back inside to help her. Not with such unwelcome suspicions clouding her mind. Quickly, she pulled on her stockings and half-boots, twisting her hair into some semblance of a chignon, after finding a collection of pins in the armoire. Not perfect, but it would do.

Sinclair stood waiting at the door, nodding in approval that she was dressed. He moved to douse the fire while Alyss glared at the enticing curve of his backside, recalling the feel of those muscles beneath her palms. "I thought you'd be in a better mood."

"I'm in a perfectly fine mood today," she retorted. "Thank you."

Could Buckmore, after refusing Sinclair payment, have then encountered him later at the stable? Suggested that ruining Alyss might be beneficial to them both? After all, Sinclair had much to gain. She was hardly likely to report him now.

Alyss turned her back on him and faced the door.

"You missed a button." His fingers brushed along her neck, breath warm. "Are you well Alyss?"

Her back wanted to arch in his direction, but Alyss wouldn't allow it. The tingle down between her breasts, she ignored. The tug of her heart, she viciously pushed aside. Alyss had known what she was doing last night. If Sinclair had taken advantage of the situation, she could hardly fault him. Alyss just hadn't thought—

"I'm quite well, Mr. Sinclair. Only ready to depart this place." She strode over to her battered parasol, the lace torn and dirty. Completely unsalvageable. But leaving it behind was out of the question. There should be no sign Alyss was ever at Buckmore's cottage.

"You need another parasol," he said quietly.

Alyss kept her features composed and chilly. "I won't go to the authorities, Sinclair, if that concerns you. Nor will I give your name to my uncle. It's quite impossible now. That should please you." Alyss smoothed down her skirts brushing off another crumb of dried mud.

"Should it?" The beard and mustache bristled as the jaw beneath all that monstrous hair drew taut.

"Well, I would think so. You've accomplished what you set

out to do. Given the events of last night, which we do not need to revisit, you should be most pleased with yourself. Any mention of you now would lead the authorities here, to Buckmore's cottage. Questions would be asked. My reputation shredded. I'm sure both you and Buckmore planned for that." Her brows drew together. "At what point did you and Mr. Elrood hatch the plan to rob me and then leave me on the road? Or was that concocted entirely by Buckmore?"

Sinclair's eyes darkened to jade. "You seriously believe—you think last night was about Buckmore?" He ran a hand through his hair, making the ends stick up. "How on earth did you convince yourself of such—"

"As I said," Alyss interrupted with a raised hand. "Last night is not something I care to revisit. Your task is complete. My lips are sealed forthwith. You need not worry I shall make anyone aware of our acquaintance. However, the same cannot be true of Buckmore. You may tell him that I still intend to report everything to my uncle. Buckmore cannot have Elizabeth."

Sinclair took a step back. "Well, isn't that lovely of you, Miss Brooks." Anger laced through each word as if she'd insulted him.

"I'm not sure what has caused your sour mood," she replied tartly. "Your little gambit last night has produced the desired results. You've no reason to be upset in the least."

"No, not in the least." He glared at Alyss a moment longer before storming outside. "Come along Miss Brooks. Time to see you safely home."

CHAPTER SEVENTEEN

*T*ERMAGANT.
    Devious fairy.

Malcolm cursed Alyss Brooks nearly a dozen different ways during the mostly silent and uneventful ride back to London. Her condescending attitude towards him had Malcolm considering tossing her off the horse. No surprise had shown on her delicate features at the sight of the animal, her only response an icy lift of one brow. Nor had Alyss objected when Malcolm lifted her up into the saddle. She kept her gaze either at the ground, or Buckmore's cottage, as if the sight of Malcolm repulsed her.

Bedding her because Buckmore required it. Had Alyss gone mad over the course of the morning?

He stared down at her slender fingers, forcibly clasped around his mid-section as they rode, refusing to deny or confirm any of her outlandish logic. Honestly, Malcolm was insulted. But he did nothing to refute her claims. Possibly, it was best if Alyss thought him completely despicable.

He couldn't have her. Not in any way that was honorable.

Even if you put aside the fact that he'd kidnapped her, Malcolm was still guilty of a great many other things. He *had* been a mercenary. Who knew if most of the doge's enemies had truly deserved their fate? At the time, Malcolm hadn't worried over it, but now those deaths weighed on him. If Alyss knew the truth, she'd be horrified. Not to mention that Malcolm was a Sinclair. A Deadly Sin. He had not a pound to his name, nor did his family.

Society reviled the Sinclairs.

What sort of life could he even offer a woman like Alyss?

Such thoughts plagued him until they arrived at the small inn on the outskirts of town. This early, the inn was quiet. No carriages milled about. Malcolm didn't think he and Alyss would draw any notice. This was as good a spot as any for them to part ways. A hack would take her to the Brooks residence. Malcolm had a small collection of coins in one pocket. Not much, but enough for Alyss.

He rode up and dismounted, watching in frustration as Alyss tried to get herself off the horse alone while still clinging to that stupid parasol, all without touching him or showing more of her calves than she wished.

"Stop." Malcolm's hands went to her waist. "I'll help you down."

"Don't touch me." She rapped his knuckles with the parasol, her distaste for him evident.

"You've been pawing me the entire trip," he snapped. "Caressing my stomach," Malcolm growled low in her ear. "Fingers straying."

This time, the battered parasol swatted him in the knee. Murder shone in her eyes. "Entirely untrue. I would sooner roll about in the muck with pigs."

"That can be arranged." Malcolm had the strongest desire to kiss her senseless, right here in full view of—he glanced around— an elderly dog and a group of pigeons. But he might never stop and that wouldn't do.

"I had no inclination to break my neck by falling off a horse," she retorted. "I assume a hack can be hailed from this place."

"I'll take care of it." He pulled forth the bit of coin he had left. Malcolm leaned over Alyss, sniffing along her skin, smelling his own scent mixed with hers. He longed to press his mouth to the spot but didn't fancy being hit with a parasol again.

Alyss had pulled the pale, nearly white strands of her hair into a loose chignon at the base of her neck. It hadn't been an entirely successful attempt. A few strands had fallen free, teasing along her cheek. He'd wrapped those pale strands around his wrist last night, bending her nearly in half as he took her from behind bent over one of Buckmore's chairs.

They'd broken the leg of that chair which Malcolm hadn't bothered to fix.

"I can hail my own hack." Those pitch black eyes glared up at him, like a starless night. Endlessly beautiful. Infinite. Malcolm wanted to drown in them. Be the last thing he ever saw.

"Take all of it, Miss Brooks." He dumped the coins in her hand. "You might have need of it." The coins were the last of what Buckmore had given him when they parted ways aboard the ship bound for Dover. Malcolm didn't have the young lord's coins. Not now. Emerson House, though likely in a sorry state, would have something in the larder and a place to lay his head. He could sell Buckmore's horse. Drew had probably had his usual luck with cards.

Her fingers closed around the coins, careful not to brush her hand against his.

"Good luck to you, Miss Brooks." There was an unsteadiness to saying goodbye to her, mainly because Malcolm didn't want to part from Alyss. He'd known it since waking up this morning with her smaller form nestled along his. He couldn't have explained why.

"I would thank you, Mr. Sinclair for bringing me back to London, but considering the circumstances I'll merely bid you an overdue farewell." Her skirts, stiff and stained with muddy water twitched in agitation as she walked towards a hack idling a short distance from the inn.

Malcolm waited, watching as she spoke to the driver who hopped down and helped her inside. The ache building inside him since watching her sleep this morning, vibrated across his chest.

Vicious little fairy.

Mounting his horse once more, Malcolm resolutely turned the animal back in the direction of Gerryhill. He had one last errand. One of the utmost importance.

CHAPTER EIGHTEEN

"ALYSS." ELIZABETH STOPPED in the foyer, a pained look on her pretty features. "You're home."

"I am. Finally." Alyss nodded to Jenks, the Brooks butler as he shut the door behind her. Brushing what dirt she could from her skirts, Alyss felt no relief at arriving to the familiar surroundings of the Brooks home, just a gnawing emptiness. As if she'd lost something important besides her virtue or the locket.

She couldn't possibly be missing Sinclair.

Pushing aside all thoughts of green eyes and broad shoulders, she reached for Elizabeth who stiffened as Alyss took her hand. An oddly reticent greeting considering her cousin had seen her kidnapped from the park and Alyss had disappeared for the night.

"I have such a tale to tell you, Elizabeth. You won't believe—"

"How could you do such a thing?" Her cousin looked at her, blue eyes filling with tears, lips trembling. "Fleeing with that stranger. Allowing me to believe you'd been abducted."

"Because I *was* abducted. But I'm home now. Where is your father?" Alyss asked feeling unsettled at Elizabeth's lack of welcome. "I must inform him of what transpired and the culprit responsible."

"Culprit?" Elizabeth shook her head, glancing back at Jenks, who was only a few feet away. "There is no need to pretend any longer," her voice lowered to barely above a whisper. "We have been informed of what actually transpired. How could you, Alyss?

I was sick with worry."

Alyss's mouth gaped open. "What actually transpired? I didn't ask to be kidnapped."

"Didn't you? You never once screamed. Nor did you struggle as you were carried away. There was no immediate request for ransom," Elizabeth stated, with a jerk of her chin. "How could you put me through all of that? I was terrified. All to find out later that it was a lie."

Alyss took a step back. "I've no idea what you're talking about. I was abducted and—"

"I was close to hysterical," Elizabeth wrenched her hand from Alyss's. "I came straight home to Papa and informed him that a strange man had taken with you." She twisted her fingers together. "Papa immediately sent for a pair of Bow Street Runners. We couldn't fathom who would wish to harm you. As I was explaining what occurred in the park to the Runners—" Elizabeth glared at her. "Lord Buckmore arrived." She wiped at the lone tear stealing down her cheek. "And I am grateful he did."

"The audacity!" Alyss exclaimed. Buckmore. The villain of this entire tale. "That's rather bold of him, considering."

"You are one to speak of bold behavior, Alyss. Thank goodness Buckmore respects Papa so much that he came straight here after leaving Gerryhill. He was as distressed as I at learning what had transpired. What he was forced to witness. You, in the company of a strange man. Your lover," Elizabeth hissed out.

The floor shifted beneath Alyss's feet. She'd been right, it seemed. Buckmore and Sinclair had plotted against her.

"That isn't true, Elizabeth," she said in a tired voice, ashamed to having been once more outmaneuvered by that despicable fop. Would there ever be an end to Buckmore's deceit? No wonder Buckmore had kept her from returning to London yesterday. He'd planned to come to Uncle Richard with his ridiculous tale before Alyss could even arrive home.

"For goodness' sake. Do you really think I have some secret lover? Why on earth would I have him abduct me from Hyde

Park and take me to Gerryhill, of all places? Wouldn't it be much easier to conduct my affair in London? Why would I go to such trouble?"

"So you admit this man is your lover." Elizabeth crossed her arms.

"There is *no lover*, Elizabeth."

At least not anymore.

Elizabeth's lips tightened into a tiny rosette. "Once Lord Buckmore related that he'd seen you with this man, saw you behaving—like a common doxy," she stumbled over the word. "The Bow Street Runners took their leave, laughing to themselves. Papa was so embarrassed. Humiliated."

If Alyss ever saw Buckmore again, she might kill him. "Don't you find it a strange coincidence that Buckmore was in Gerryhill? The lone witness to my transgression? Alyss snapped at her. "He's lying, Elizabeth. Once you hear the entire story, you'll understand."

Elizabeth's cheeks colored. "Papa said the same thing, that was when Buckmore admitted the rest—he suggested that you planned the entire affair to gain his attention." She bit her lip and looked away. "That you had long harbored feelings for him and your—dislike was nothing more than that of a scorned woman. Because his affection is for me." She thumped her chest.

Had the situation not been so dire, Alyss might have burst into laughter. But Elizabeth was entirely serious. "Let me understand, Buckmore came here to tell you that I had myself kidnapped by my lover, but then followed Buckmore to Gerryhill out of jealousy, I suppose, because I'm truly in love with *him*?"

"You wanted his attention," Elizabeth stammered. "He told me once Papa left the room how you've pursued him for months, no matter how he's rejected you. All this time you kept me and Buckmore apart because you—" she looked away. "Wanted him for yourself."

Alyss made a sound of disbelief. "You can't be serious. How would I even know Buckmore was in Gerryhill?" She shook her head. "I find Buckmore deplorable. Every word he spouts is a lie. Let me guess, after laying everything out so neatly, he asked if he could court you once more."

"He suggested it." Elizabeth gave her a mutinous look. "Now that I am aware of the truth. How you tried to poison me against him despite his love for me."

"You wish to wed Buckmore?" Alyss held up her hands, astounded at her cousin's absolute blindness where Buckmore was concerned. "Fine. I'm tired of trying to dissuade you. But before you accept his courtship, allow me to apprise you of his noble nature. The man who took me from the park yesterday was hired to abduct you. He took me by accident. Buckmore planned to compromise you at Gerryhill and then return to London and force Uncle Richard to agree to your marriage. Are those the actions of a devoted gentleman?"

"I don't believe you." Elizabeth's eyes welled with tears. "He loves me. He's said so."

"A man you've known less than six months. But me, your cousin who has been devoted to you since birth, you can believe I would lie to you. That I have taken a lover, asked him to abduct me from the park, then have said lover take me to Gerryhill, on the chance Buckmore was there, for the sole purpose of making him jealous? Listen to yourself, Elizabeth." Alyss gritted her teeth. "Buckmore is lying. He wants your dowry. He's counting on the fact that you are—"

"Stupid?" Elizabeth sobbed. "Poor, half-witted Elizabeth. Pretty. Wealthy. But so grievously unintelligent that her vastly superior cousin must protect her. Because no one is as brilliant as Alyss Brooks. She is always right. About everything. I'm surprised I can even feed myself without your instruction."

Shocked by the vehemence in her cousin's tone, Alyss reached for her once more. "I was going to say stubborn."

"Don't spare me, Alyss." Her cousin wiped at her cheek. "I know I am only ten thousand pounds wrapped up in ribbon and silk. I suppose there is no other reason a gentleman like Buckmore might pursue me but my dowry, and the fact I look fetching in pink." She sniffed and looked away. "Poor, stupid Elizabeth."

"I only ever want what is best for you," Alyss said quietly, her heart breaking. "And it is not Buckmore. He is impoverished by his own hand. I do not believe he genuinely loves you."

Another sob left her cousin.

"I'm sorry." Alyss had wanted Elizabeth to see the truth, but not like this. "He has not been honorable."

Elizabeth looked down at the floor, unwilling to look Alyss in the eye. "You should speak to my father. If what you say is true—"

"It is," Alyss pleaded.

"Then I am not the only one Buckmore has said such things to. Papa was very distressed when he returned from his club last night. Now, if you will excuse me, I believe I will go upstairs and lie down." She retreated in the direction of the stairs, her slender shoulders shaking with unshed tears.

Damn Buckmore.

He'd concocted some mad tale that painted Alyss in an un-friendly light. Half the neighbors had probably seen the Bow Street Runners arrive to the Brooks' home. The talk of sour spinster Alyss Brooks, her mysterious lover and fake kidnapping was likely already making the rounds if she knew Buckmore. Alyss didn't doubt it would be believed. Society loved nothing so much as scandal.

A shiver ran down her frame, making Alyss clutch at her ruined skirts. She took a step forward, feeling the pull of her muscles, a reminder of the previous night.

She *had* taken a lover at Gerryhill. That was the only part of Buckmore's tale that was remotely close to the truth. She could still smell Sinclair on her skin. Feel his lips on hers. The things she'd allowed—

Alyss didn't want to believe that Sinclair would be a party to seducing her on Buckmore's command, but what else could she assume? The lengths that scurrilous fop had gone to in order to discredit Alyss was astounding, but she'd threatened him with exposure. His own ruination. She should have known Buckmore would find a way to strike back. Last night *could* have been planned by him. And who was to say that the two men hadn't met once more as Buckmore left Gerryhill and convinced Sinclair to do his bidding once more?

The thought left an ugly stain inside Alyss.

The accusations she'd hurled at Sinclair this morning in her unsettled state now seemed more real than ever in light of Buckmore's timely and pointed conversation with Uncle Richard. Still, she couldn't summon up an ounce of regret for last night.

Alyss had felt wanted, for the first time in her life. Desirable. She didn't want that to be a lie.

Her shoulders sagged in exhaustion. She would feel better after a bath. A pot of tea. Something to eat. Then she would face her uncle.

"Alyss." Uncle Richard strolled out of his study. "I thought I heard your voice." There was an edge to her uncle's words which instantly made her wary. A snifter of brandy was held aloft in his hand, though it was only the middle of the day. His sandy hair, usually neatly styled, was sticking up around his ears as if he'd run his fingers through the strands in agitation. "Would you join me please?"

Uncle Richard, for all that he and Mrs. Hitchcock were quite obviously more than friends who enjoyed tea together, was a bit staid. Alyss's father, Nolan, had been the exact opposite. Uncle Richard was steady. Firm. Careful with his reputation and that of his family. And he had been a real father to her, treating Alyss with love and affection. And now she'd disappointed him.

"Of course." She obediently moved towards her uncle's study.

Uncle Richard waved her inside, concern flitting over his usually jovial features as his gaze landed on the water-stained dress and ruined parasol.

"I am relieved you are home." He cleared his throat, brow wrinkling, uncertain how to broach the subject before them.

Uncle Richard looked more confused than angry. His eyes kept flitting to the muddy hem of her dress and the mess of her hair.

"I am well, uncle, considering I was abducted from the park yesterday morning." Alyss lifted her chin, daring him to disbelieve her as Elizabeth had. "I understand that Lord Buckmore," she didn't bother to hide her disdain, "felt it necessary to comment on my disappearance. How convenient of him."

Uncle Richard's mouth drew together. "He claims to have seen you at Gerryhill with an unknown gentleman." Two spots of pink stood out on his cheeks the conversation far more unsettling for him than Alyss. "Elizabeth was hysterical at seeing you tossed over a strange man's shoulder. I summoned Bow Street Runners as I was in fear for your life."

Alyss nodded. "Elizabeth informed me."

His brow wrinkled once more. "A kidnapping with no ransom demanded and one in which you neither struggled nor screamed for help. According to Lord Buckmore you were abducted by your lover as a means to cover your dalliance."

"The gentleman in question is not my lover, but a mercenary hired by Buckmore to take Elizabeth." Alyss didn't lie. Sinclair *had* been her lover, but no longer. "He mistook me for her." She waved her hand. "Not very observant, I grant you. We look nothing alike. I didn't struggle because Buckmore's man assured me that Lord Buckmore was waiting for him. And me. Well, Elizabeth."

"I see." Uncle Richard waved a hand for Alyss to sit.

"Elizabeth has told me of Buckmore's visit. Tell me, could he explain how I would even know he was at Gerryhill?"

"No, he was unable to do so to my satisfaction. I found the entire tale preposterous, given your dislike of Buckmore, which I know to be true. Also, I do not think you capable of such deceit."

"Thank you. Elizabeth does not share your faith in me." It was a relief to know Uncle Richard didn't believe Buckmore. She sank into the cushions of the sofa, grateful for that much at least.

"I would hear your version of events."

"I was at Gerryhill," Alyss said carefully. "Taken there by the man hired to kidnap Elizabeth. As I said, I did not struggle or try to escape once I realized Buckmore was behind the entire affair."

Uncle Richard made a resigned, frustrated sound. "And why is that, Alyss?"

"I was right about Buckmore," she offered instead.

"Answer the question. Why did you allow yourself to be abducted in Elizabeth's place?"

Her uncle knew her so well. He already knew the answer. "I wanted to confront Buckmore myself. Tell him of his failure to trap Elizabeth in marriage. I hit him with my parasol."

Uncle Richard pinched the bridge of his nose. He rose and went to the sideboard, refilling his snifter of brandy. "Splendid. You assaulted a lord. What did Buckmore do once he realized the mistake?"

Alyss studied the hem of her dress. "Stranded me in Gerryhill. I foolishly assumed he was enough of a gentleman to at least allow me to sit atop the carriage with his driver, but that was an incorrect assumption. At the time, I thought only of confronting Buckmore."

"There is a time to be right Alyss, and a time to be wise."

"I was trying to be both. I—wanted to prove that Buckmore's intentions towards Elizabeth weren't at all honorable." She did not tell Uncle Richard how Buckmore had bribed Mr. Elrood to ensure that Alyss not leave Gerryhill. Or that Elrood had robbed Alyss. She'd already paid the price for her arrogance with the loss of her mother's locket. "The rain started. I couldn't get back to London. Buckmore has a cottage in Gerryhill." Alyss cringed when another bit of mud fell off the hem of her dress. "I—stayed the night there and managed to find a driver to bring me home today."

Uncle Richard stared at her for some moments until Alyss was forced to look away. Her hands twisted on the handle of the parasol.

"This must stop, Alyss," Uncle Richard said quietly. "Putting yourself at risk purely to prove Buckmore an unprincipled rake is unacceptable. You could have been hurt," his voice broke. "Or worse. I have been worried sick over you."

"I'm sorry, Uncle." Alyss felt horrible that he'd worried over her. She hadn't thought past Buckmore, nor the true repercussions of her actions.

"You will be relieved to know that I once again refused Buckmore's request to court Elizabeth. I'm well aware of the sort of man he is, one with little honor and even less wealth. His tale was outlandish. His appearance too convenient. You are not the only one with a brain in the Brooks household."

Alyss bit her lip, duly chastised. She hadn't realized—how condescending she'd become. "I only wanted to protect Elizabeth."

"Now it is you we must worry over." Her uncle's tone grew grim. "Buckmore took my refusal hardly better than he did the first time. He had hoped his preposterous tale would make me reconsider his proposal, but it did not. Jenks overheard him curse you as he departed. I will assume he is the culprit behind the sordid gossip swirling about you. Buckmore is incredibly petty. He is determined to discredit you and destroy your reputation."

"But I was *kidnapped*," Alyss asserted. "Taken against my will."

"Yes, but you didn't scream. Or struggle to get away. I've heard that detail repeated half a dozen times at my club last night." Uncle Richard gave her a resigned look. "Society will choose to believe Buckmore's version of events because it suits them. You don't have a great many friends, Alyss."

"I suppose," she replied bitterly, "had I thrown myself from a moving carriage and broken my neck, my innocence would be assured."

Uncle Richard gave her a sympathetic look. "What happened to this hired thug of Buckmore's?" her uncle asked.

Alyss stilled. "I've no idea. After I confronted Buckmore he— well, he disappeared." Sinclair might be in London right now, perhaps sharing a drink with Buckmore and laughing over Alyss's new predicament.

Uncle Richard searched her features for the longest time. "I'm well aware of Buckmore's cottage. He used to keep a—young lady there." He rolled his shoulders. "Mrs. Hitchcock relayed the details to me. I assume that is where you spent the night."

"I did. The cottage was open. It was either that or the stables down the road."

Uncle Richard nodded. "Agreed. You were alone?"

"Yes," Alyss lied. "Buckmore had stocked the cottage anticipating Elizabeth being there. There was food. Wood for the fire. I was quite comfortable waiting for the storm to pass."

Heat pricked her cheeks and she took in her parasol, running her fingers over the tattered lace.

"You really hit Buckmore with that?"

"Numerous times. He squealed like a child. Fop." Alyss gave her uncle a weak smile.

Panic blossomed inside her, great tendrils of it leeching into her skin. Alyss may not have many friends, or any at all, but she did have a reputation. How everyone must be laughing that staid spinster and companion to her cousin, scourge of liberty-taking gentlemen everywhere, Alyss Brooks was now some sort of a lightskirt.

I'll kill Buckmore.

"Kidnapped or not, you spent a great deal of time in the company of a stranger in a closed carriage. I wish you had considered your reputation more than confronting Buckmore. I realize you are well past the age of consent. You've chosen to stay unwed, and I've respected your decision. I know your father's poor decisions affected you in ways I don't think Nolan anticipated." He patted her hand, worry for her etched in his features. "Love did not destroy your mother," her uncle said quietly. "Keeping yourself from it, avoiding affection will only cause you misery, I think."

Tears welled in Alyss's eyes. Uncle Richard rarely spoke of

her parents. Nor had he ever broached this topic with her. "I do not need to marry to be happy. I am content with my life," she said firmly.

Uncle Richard nodded slowly. "Marriage for other reasons might suit you, Alyss."

Another wave of panic struck her. "Why are we discussing this now?"

"We have no way to prove your story, Alyss. Accusations such as kidnapping, leveled at a peer, are difficult at best. As I said, you have few friends in society, certainly none who will come to your aid. If the gossip grows louder, I'm afraid you cannot accompany Elizabeth about or act as chaperone. Mrs. Hitchcock has offered to help in your stead."

"Is this punishment? I thought you believed me."

"I do. But the talk at my club last evening was quite— *unsavory*, Alyss. And it has only just begun. I feel I should be honest about that."

"What happens," her voice was barely above a whisper. "If the gossip doesn't die down? Will you send me away?" Her hand pressed against her stomach. In truth, that might not be so terrible. Alyss could imagine herself with a cat or two in a seaside cottage, reliving her foolish but pleasurable night with Sinclair.

"That is why I broach the subject of marriage. It would be a solution to the difficulties you find yourself in." He took a deep breath. "I know of your reticence, but perhaps you could approach my suggestion as merely a business arrangement. Or for companionship only. Friendship, perhaps."

Alyss thought she might be ill. "Would you mind overmuch, Uncle, if I availed myself of a glass of ratafia?"

"Brandy will do more good, Alyss." He once more went to the sideboard and poured Alyss out a thimbleful of brandy before handing the glass into her trembling hand.

"If the talk continues, you won't be received. Walking in the park will have other women crossing the path to avoid you. No more escorting Elizabeth about, you won't even be able to be seen in her company."

Alyss swallowed down the brandy. "May I have more, please?" How often had she warned Elizabeth of such things? Examples of what could happen should she be compromised by some randy gentleman. How ironic that it should be Alyss who'd been ruined.

Uncle Richard refilled her glass. "Mr. Clinton desires a match with you. I cannot force you to wed him, but he is an option."

"It isn't fair," she said, swallowing the brandy. "I've done nothing wrong."

"No, it is not."

Uncle Richard slid closer and placed an arm around Alyss's shoulder, pulling her into the familiar scent of his pipe tobacco and shaving soap. Just as he had when she was a child and newly arrived in London, still in shock over her mother's death.

A sob left her. And then another. Alyss dropped the parasol. And cried as she hadn't since then.

CHAPTER NINETEEN

MALCOLM'S NOSE WRINKLED at the stink of sex, unwashed bodies, and Elrood's breath passing between his cracked lips. Luckily, the man slept like the dead. Cocking the pistol, he placed the end directly on the sleeping man's forehead.

The deceitful gig driver from Gerryhill wasn't difficult to find. Honestly, just sniffing the air alerted you to the man's presence in the vicinity.

Elrood was ensconced in a tiny brothel not a half-hour's ride in the opposite direction of Buckmore's cottage in a rather unforgettable place named Wayburn. A group of scantily clad women had sauntered around Malcolm while he stated his business, at which point a gruff, overly muscled lout tried to throw him out the back door. But after breaking the man's nose and one of his fingers, Malcolm had been pointed up the stairs. Room Five.

The door was locked, but that hardly presented a problem.

The buxom young lady sleeping next to Elrood roused when Malcolm approached, mouth opening to scream before he quickly placed his palm over her lips.

"Not a sound. Never shot a woman. Don't intend for you to be the first."

Her bloodshot eyes focused on him as she took a shaky breath, drawing his attention to her enormous bosom, and what lay nestled between her breasts. Alyss's locket.

"Hand that over," he nodded to the necklace. "Doesn't belong to you. Nor him."

The woman shook her head in refusal, the snarl of her dirty brown curls snaking over her shoulders.

"Fine." Malcolm reached down with the hand holding the pistol and snatched the locket from her. Alyss's treasured necklace had been given to some doxy so Elrood could spend a pleasant afternoon. It made Malcolm hate the stableman even more. "I'm going to lift my hand. If you so much as blow out a puff of air," he growled softly. "I'll shoot you and ruin my perfect record. Get out."

Nodding enthusiastically, she rolled off the bed, not bothering to cover herself, grabbed her robe, and backed out of the room. Once downstairs, she'd probably cause a ruckus. He hadn't made friends below. Best to get this over with.

Alyss's smart little reticule lay discarded in the corner, whatever coin it may have contained long gone. No sign of her bonnet. But at least he'd found the locket. He pushed the end of the pistol harder into Elrood's forehead. When that didn't wake the sleeping man, Malcolm stuck the pistol up one of the stableman's nostrils.

Elrood cursed and swatted at the other side of the bed. He tried to move his head and found he couldn't. Bleary eyes opened to take in Malcolm.

"Sweet Jesus."

"Afraid not," Malcolm quipped. "But don't worry, you'll be seeing him soon. Well," he shrugged. "You're likely to go in the other direction."

"You—" Elrood trembled, struggling to cover up the pathetic bit of flesh between his legs. "Just take the damned horse."

"Already did." Malcolm shoved the pistol further into the man's nose, making sure it hurt. "I'm here to discuss your talent at robbing defenseless women and leaving them stranded during a rainstorm."

Elrood paled. He stopped trying to cover up the worm dangling between his legs.

"I was paid to do it." He choked as Malcolm twisted the end of the pistol. "Lord Buckmore didn't want her getting back to London right away. I don't know why." He cringed before grabbing at Malcolm's arms in a poor attempt to wrest away the gun.

Malcolm sat on him, not bothering to hide his disgust at having the man's cock touching him. "No wonder you had to bribe your companion to fuck you with a locket. Is that a bloody maggot you've got there? Certainly isn't a cock."

Elrood thrashed about. "His lordship said I could take something for my trouble. And she was trouble. Wouldn't shut up."

He was going to murder Buckmore. Probably spend the rest of his life in Newgate. It would be worth it. "Did you touch her?"

"No." Elrood's eyes went wide in terror as Malcolm's fingers pressed into his neck. "God, no. She ain't the sort of woman I like."

"Lucky for you. But you did leave her on the side of the road. In a thunderstorm. After robbing her. Reason enough for me to relieve the world of your presence, Elrood."

Elrood started to sob. A glob of snot worked its way out of his nose.

Malcolm's lip curled in disgust.

"Lord Buckmore. He—just wanted to make sure she didn't get to London ahead of him. His lordship wanted me to shoot you, but I didn't, did I?"

"That doesn't make us friends." Buckmore was more cunning than Malcolm had given him credit for. He'd never had any intention of paying Malcolm, but instead was going to have him shot by this idiot. How neat and tidy. Too bad it hadn't worked out for His Lordship. As he'd soon find out.

Malcolm pulled the pistol back and pushed off Elrood. "If I see you again, especially in London, I'll shoot that," he jerked the pistol in the direction of Elrood's quivering cock. "Right off." He sidled out of the room, not bothering to shut the door.

As he suspected, downstairs was in an uproar. The man's nose he broke was waving about a pistol.

Malcolm stomped right over to him, took the pistol from the man's hand, and hit the butt against the lout's already broken nose. "I'll just take this. Safer for everyone."

Several pairs of eyes watched Malcolm as he departed, but no one dared to stop him. Jumping on his horse, he turned the animal back down the road, towards London. Once he was a good distance away and assured no one was stupid enough to pursue him, Malcolm reached inside the pocket of his coat, running the edge of his thumb across the small gold oval of Alyss's locket. He slowed and opened the locket. Tucked inside were pictures of a man and a woman.

Alyss did indeed have her father's nose. There was an inscription on the back, the small letters almost impossible to read.

Wherever you go, I will follow.

Apt, Malcolm thought, considering Alyss's mother had obviously died following her husband about places not fit for an Englishwoman with child. He understood the sentiment, if not the exact feeling. His own mother had been nothing more than a shell after the death of Malcolm's father, Lord Emerson. And after Alyss—the seed of that feeling was there, nestled in Malcolm's chest. Impossible in such a short time, but there it was.

Malcolm had held his mother's hand as she died. He'd cursed Bentley and Lady Longwood, for sending the Sinclairs to Dunnings. Because Dunnings made Mother *want* to leave—all of them. Not even her children could keep her on this earth. She wanted to follow Malcolm's father. Grief, as much as the blood filling her lungs, had killed her.

There had never been a question of whether or not he should retrieve the locket for Alyss. Nothing could have kept him from doing so, no matter how unwise it would be to see her again.

When he'd carried Alyss, exhausted and spent, to the bed at Buckmore's cottage last night, her hair had streamed over his hands like moonbeams. He'd tucked her beneath the quilt and slid in behind her, listening as her breathing evened out, her body sheltered alongside his. The rain had stopped, and Malcolm knew he should go retrieve the horse. But Alyss and her warmth kept him close. Finally unable to delay any longer, Malcolm pressed a kiss to one naked breast before heading out into the night, to the stable to steal back the damned horse which was promised to him to begin with.

Honestly, if Buckmore survived the year it would be a miracle.

When he returned, it wasn't yet dawn. He looked at the settee and then back at the still sleeping Alyss. Malcolm had never spent the entire night with a woman. Never slept beside one. But the urge to lay curled around her forced him back to the bed. She sighed and pushed her bottom up against his aching cock.

He'd considered simply abducting her again, but this time, he'd keep her.

The confusion over that thought, among a host of others, had him putting distance between them when she woke. Malcolm couldn't just abduct her, not again, and he knew it. What sort of life could he offer? And he had no idea of her feelings on the subject.

Pressing his thumb over the words on the locket once more, he found himself longing for Alyss.

Beautiful, vicious, little fairy.

He urged the horse forward. In a different world, one in which he hadn't met Buckmore, and he wasn't a mercenary from a disgraced family, Malcolm might have become acquainted with Miss Alyss Brooks properly. But given the nature of their acquaintance, he doubted she would ever allow him near her again. Alyss was under the assumption Malcolm had bedded her last night to keep her from reporting him to the authorities. And worse, she suspected he was in league with that idiot, Buckmore. If Malcolm were stupid enough to approach Alyss, she was just as likely to shout for the authorities as kiss him. Lady Longwood, terrible maternal aunt of the late, unlamented Bentley Sinclair, would sail forward as a character witness at Malcom's trial, ensuring his demise.

Perhaps he could send Alyss the locket anonymously. No note. Nothing to identify him. But Malcolm wasn't sure he could do that. He wanted to see her. Touch her. Keep her.

Dammit.

CHAPTER TWENTY

A FTER ANOTHER HOUR of riding, Malcolm finally arrived on Bruton Street, just as the sun was beginning to set. Handing the reins of his horse to a gawking footman, Malcolm took a moment to take in Emerson House. The London residence of his family looked exactly as it had all those years ago, right down to the front door with the curved knocker.

"Tradesmen go round the back." The footman near the steps, one who his brother shouldn't have been able to afford given the family's circumstances, tried unsuccessfully to direct him elsewhere.

Malcolm snarled at him.

The lad scurried away, probably running to report Malcolm's presence and call for reinforcements. Cleaning up a bit before arriving wouldn't have been remiss, but he hadn't had the opportunity. He probably looked like a savage if the peering of the neighbor across the street through her laced curtains was any indication, but he thought his time had been better spent getting the locket back for Alyss.

Lady Mayfield.

The name of the woman studying him from the safety of her drawing room window popped into Malcolm's head, if indeed the Mayfields still lived on Bruton Street. Lady Mayfield would never receive Malcolm's mother and she had been unkind to Tamsin. He hoped the return of the Sinclairs was giving Lady Mayfield fits.

Malcolm smiled and waved at the house across the street.

The curtain fell back.

He dearly hoped Tamsin was strutting about London in breeches and riding astride. At the very least he envisioned his older sister had punched a lecherous gentleman or two while Drew fleeced them at cards.

Alyss would look splendid in a pair of breeches, twirling that bloody parasol.

Malcolm was so engrossed thinking of Alyss he hadn't yet lifted the knocker and barely turned at the sound of a carriage pulling up before Emerson House.

A well-sprung, horribly expensive carriage with an unknown coat of arms blazoned across the door. Fine horses. A driver and two grooms. The carriage door swung open to reveal a large, slightly disheveled gentleman who proceeded to lumber up the front steps. He shot Malcolm a snooty, arrogant look as he approached. Based on the way the footmen were rushing out of Emerson House to bow, almost scraping their noses against the ground, this visitor must be of some import.

Not a bill collector, then. That was a relief.

A pair of cool, silver eyes slid over Malcolm with disdain. The giant made a sound in his chest as they stared at each other.

"Tradesmen or beggars," the big man intoned, with one snide raise of a brow. "Do not use the front entrance."

Pompous prick.

"I live here," Malcolm stated somewhat defensively.

A derisive snort. Then another sound, like a disturbed bear being awakened, came from beside Malcolm. The snob leaned from his much greater height, cocked his head, and peered directly into Malcolm's face. His eyes widened. Something resembling a grin tugged at his lips.

"Malcolm Sinclair." The giant straightened. "How unexpected."

"Aren't you going to knock?" Malcolm spat, unnerved he'd been so easily recognized by a gentleman he obviously didn't know.

"I don't need to," Malcolm was informed in a lofty tone. "Holly, Emerson's butler, would have noted my arrival. I'm here to retrieve my wife. Perhaps sup."

Arrogant bastard.

"Good for you." He pitied whoever was wed to this titled twit. The lady in question must be acquainted with one of Malcolm's sisters. Which meant they'd made some friends since the last time Malcolm had been in London.

"I am Ware." The giant gave him a sideways glance.

"Ware who?" Malcolm was tired. Hungry. Dirty, to be sure. And there was a strange longing in his chest for a girl he hardly knew. The last thing he cared about was who this idiot happened to be or his wife.

"The Duke of Ware." He raised his brows in astonishment. "You don't know who I am."

"Nor do I care." Malcolm remembered his manners. "Your Grace." Hadn't Buckmore mentioned this duke?

Ware made a noise in his throat.

The door swung open to reveal a man with the build of a prizefighter and fists the size of cabbages. He took in the duke and bowed immediately.

"Holly," the duke intoned pleasantly. "I'm here to retrieve my duchess."

"Of course, Your Grace. My apologies for the delay in coming to the door." The butler straightened and moved to the side. "One of the footmen was up in arms because some sort of vagrant," he glared, finally taking note of Malcolm, "was at the door. Masonry work starts tomorrow. Use the back door when you return."

Mason? I look like a bloody mason?

"I thought him to be an ox-cart driver at first," Ware said over his shoulder as he marched over the tile foyer. "But even so, that is Malcolm Sinclair."

"Malcolm Sinclair." The butler's eyes widened as he bowed

once more. "Mr. Sinclair, but we weren't expecting you so soon. I believe the family has been wagering on whether you would arrive at all." Holly's lips pursed. "What I mean to say is—" He turned to whistle.

A maid, skirts flapping about, came flying around the corner. She bobbed politely.

"Please prepare a room for Mr. Sinclair and inform Lord Emerson of his brother's early arrival."

"I said I would be here in time for Aurora's debut," Malcolm said under his breath.

Holly's head snapped up. "Oh, you haven't missed it, Mr. Sinclair. The ball is at the end of the week."

"Held at my lavish home." Ware smirked. "The dowager duchess is sponsoring Lady Aurora." He sailed past both Malcolm and Holly and strode in the direction of the drawing room. "Your sister will be annoyed I'm so late. I did warn her. *Lucanus cervus* require extensive study."

"Luca—wait, you are hosting a ball for Aurora. Is your wife a friend of the family?" How had the Deadly Sins managed to wiggle their way into the graces of a duke?

"You aren't paying attention. The rest of your family is so intelligent, I'd no idea you wouldn't be. Seems odd."

Offended, Malcolm's hands curled into fists. "Now wait just a bloody—"

Holly ran ahead of them, stopping only to open the doors of the drawing room with a flourish. "His Grace, the Duke of Ware, and Mr. Malcolm Sinclair."

Ware stepped inside immediately.

Malcolm hesitated. The last time he had been in that room, indeed in this house, had been to bury his father. Tamsin had thrown something with jelly at Lady Longwood. Malcolm had beat up Percival, Lady Longwood's horrid son, while Drew tossed tiny biscuits at the woman's daughters. He closed his eyes for a second, seeing himself and his siblings as children, running through this house and terrorizing London. Mother fading into the settee, weeping as Bentley ordered them all to Dunnings.

He took a hesitant step forward.

The first thing Malcolm saw was the portrait of his parents above the fireplace, he stared up at their happy faces, an ache for them both hitting him firmly in the stomach.

"Malcolm."

A gorgeous creature, hair a collection of curls and bows, dressed in deep blue silk with sapphires dangling from her ears, rushed across the room.

He blinked, nearly too shocked to speak. "Tamsin?"

"Of course, it's me, you idiot." She punched him hard on the shoulder before enveloping Malcolm in a warm, jasmine-scented embrace.

When he'd last seen his sister, she'd been storming about in torn trousers, filthy boots with the soles falling off, and smelling of horse.

Ware watched him with a smug look, before turning a lovestruck gaze at Tamsin.

Oh, bloody hell.

"I told you a surprise would follow me in," Ware intoned. He'd managed to wedge his large form into one of the chairs which protested dramatically.

"Yes," Malcolm's sister answered. "But I thought you'd discovered a new species of beetle." She waved her hands. "Not my missing brother."

"No one found me," Malcolm grumbled. "I was standing on the front step."

Tamsin gave Malcolm one final squeeze before sauntering over to Ware. She trailed her fingers brazenly along Ware's shoulder before pressing a kiss to his cheek in full view of Malcolm. "You seem surprised. You did get my letter, did you not?" she said to Malcolm. "This is my duke. Ware."

A blush stood out on the duke's cheeks, alarming in a man of his size and stature. "I am." He gazed back at Tamsin with utter adoration. "Your duke."

"No—" Malcolm stuttered. "The last letter I received mentioned Jordan might have to wed an heiress, but nothing at all about you—and you're married to him?" He gestured at Ware.

"I am." She brushed something that looked like a leaf from Ware's arm. "Don't worry, your shock mirrors that of most of London. Lady Longwood in particular has had quite an upset, hasn't she, Ware?"

"A possible fit of apoplexy when she spotted us at the theater."

"Don't worry, she still disparages the Sinclairs as often as possible, but more quietly. Poor Odessa came with her own scandal, which delighted the sour hag, but Odessa is Ware's cousin and insulting a duke's relation is frowned upon. Her aunt, Miss Maplehurst, is Aurora's chaperone." Tamsin paused, thankfully, because she was making Malcolm's head hurt. "You haven't had a letter since I wrote to you that Jordan might have to wed an heiress?" Tamsin lips drew together. She didn't look happy. "I should have known when you didn't reply after the letter about Dunnings. Jordan said you were merely too taciturn or busy shooting at people to show how overjoyed you must be. But I could hardly merit it."

"I moved around quite a bit. Spain, Geneva, then Venice for some time until I left the service of the doge. I was in France until recently, but circumstances forced me to leave rather unexpectedly. Your letters never reached me. I'm sorry, Tamsin."

His fingers slid into his pocket, trailing over Alyss's locket once more.

"A pity. There was quite a lot to tell you." Tamsin was leaning over the duke, smiling at him and smoothing his coat.

Malcolm watched them in rapt horror. What had Ware *done* to Tamsin? His sister was—*cooing* over the duke. Dewy eyed. It was rather unnerving. He cleared his throat. "Where is everyone?"

"Oh, I imagine Holly's gone to get them. Ware had his beetles today, so I accompanied Aurora to the modiste. Finishing touches on her ball gown and all that." She held up something between her fingers. "Good lord, is that a wing from something?"

Ware shrugged "Possibly." At Malcolm's look he said, "I'm an entomologist."

Malcolm had no idea what the duke was talking about. "An ento—"

"It means he studies insects," Jordan said from the doorway, dressed finer than Malcolm had ever seen him. But it wasn't only the clothing that was shocking, but Jordan's manner. There was a lightness about his older brother, as if the enormous responsibility of the Deadly Sins no longer weighed so heavily.

He's happy.

Jordan took three big steps and pulled Malcolm into a hearty embrace. "I thought Holly had been nipping at the brandy again when he told me you were here."

The butler, who stood at attention just outside the drawing room, murmured, "I prefer Irish whiskey now, my lord."

"Ah, yes. My mistake, Holly." Jordan took in Malcolm. "You do look disreputable, Mal. Good God. Look at your beard." Jordan turned Malcolm back and forth. "And your hair. I nearly didn't recognize you."

"He did." Malcolm nodded in annoyance at the duke. "Which was a bit unsettling."

"I'm observant," Ware intoned. "Unlike my duchess. I informed Holly that this was indeed your brother, Emerson. Not someone in search of scraps from the kitchen. Though I believe he's hungry. I can hear his stomach grumbling from over here. It was the eyes," Ware continued. "Same as Andrew's. Oh, and he smells of horse."

Malcolm decided at some point he would punch Ware right in his perfect nose. Honestly, he was surprised Tamsin hadn't yet.

"A bath would not be remiss." Jordan's nose wrinkled.

"I've only just arrived," Malcolm snapped back. "I *have* been on a bloody horse all day. I'm a bit travel-stained." He glared at the duke. "And I haven't been offered any refreshments. We do have refreshments, do we not?"

"We do." Jordan nodded at Holly. The overly large butler disappeared in an instant.

"Where did you find him? A boxing ring?" The Sinclairs hadn't had a butler since their father's death. It would take some getting used to.

Jordan strolled over to the sidebar, which was not only filled with a large selection of decanters, but also fine-cut crystal glasses. Something they'd never had at Dunnings. Only chipped teacups and some battered pewter mugs.

"I found him," Tamsin said, her eyes sparkling. "I don't think Holly was ever a prizefighter, though he'd make a fine one. His appearance deters unwelcome visitors, as Lady Longwood found out."

Malcolm took in the rich furnishings as Jordan thrust a glass into his waiting hand. The Sinclairs had a butler *and* footmen. Maids. He hadn't been paying attention earlier. The house smelled like beeswax. Tamsin was wed to a duke.

"We are no longer impoverished," he said to no one in particular. "Are we?" The truth was before him. He'd moved about so much that Malcolm had missed more than one letter from his family, it seemed.

"Not even a little bit," Jordan assured him. "There is coal at Dunnings."

Malcolm coughed. "I beg your pardon?" Dunnings had been a horrible, cold, barren place. A long-forgotten estate, as far away from London as Bentley could send them. The idea that anything of value could come from Dunnings was—"Coal?"

"A great load of it. Might be the largest deposit in all of England according to the geologist we've engaged. Father knew, or at least, he was investigating the possibility at the time of his death. It's a long story." Jordan lifted his glass. "But suffice it to say the Sinclairs are now a family of means."

If he had known, if Malcolm had received the news of his family's good fortunes, he might never have agreed to Buckmore's mad scheme. The young lord had surely known that the Sinclairs were no longer impoverished. Knew Tamsin was wed to the Duke of Ware, which was why he'd mentioned the name. And deliberately didn't tell Malcolm.

He should have pushed that little prick into the ocean during the crossing to Dover.

But I wouldn't have met Alyss.

"Mal?" Jordan placed a hand on his shoulder. "I know it's a lot to take in. There are times when I wake up in a panic, worried that Bentley is still alive and knows about Dunnings. That he'll bankrupt us all once more. Sit down. Your room is being made ready. Holly will bring something to eat."

Odessa, Jordan's wife, arrived shortly thereafter, exclaiming over Malcolm before introducing the older woman at her side, Miss Maplehurst. By the time Drew finally made his appearance, sauntering into the room as if he owned it, dressed in an expensive coat and looking every inch a London gentleman, Malcolm barely registered any shock at the admiration Odessa's aunt displayed for his backside and shoulders.

"Mal."

His charming, graceful twin. Handsome in an aristocratic way that had somehow completely skipped Jordan and Malcolm. As he strode across the room, all Malcolm could think was that Drew looked exactly like their father.

His brother stood perfectly still before him, then in unison, he and Malcolm both dipped their chins, pressing their foreheads together. A holdover from when they were children and rarely, if ever, apart.

"You've been gone a very long time and you smell of horse," Drew whispered. "There might be a crumb stuck in that beard. You haven't stabbed anyone lately, have you?"

"I worried you might have been shot over a game of cards," Malcom whispered back. "Or by a jealous husband. I did threaten a man just this morning, does that count?"

Drew straightened, smiling in his amiable way. "No more

jealous husbands for me. Or widows, save the one. Just fields of potatoes and cabbages. Didn't you receive any of my letters?"

"He didn't even know about Dunnings," Tamsin crowed from across the room, practically sitting in Ware's lap. "Or that I'd become a duchess."

"Yes, well. That's a little hard for all of us to take in, Tamsin." Drew rolled his eyes. "Had Lady Longwood been able to throw herself at the bishop during your wedding to stop the proceedings, I have no doubt she would have done so." He leaned over. "A bit of advice, whatever you do, don't allow Odessa," he nodded to Jordan's honey-haired wife, "To make a wax mask of your face until after you've shaved. And if she starts to relate the tale of the German baker, ask her to stop."

"Odessa?" Malcolm had only just met Jordan's wife, but he'd found her lovely and very welcoming. "Why would she want to pour wax on my face?"

"Trust me on this, Mal. I still have nightmares about it."

A commotion at the front of the room drew everyone's attention. "I didn't believe Holly." A ball of pink silk streamed into the drawing room, butting Malcolm in the chest, nearly causing him to spill the whiskey. "I *knew* you would come home for my debut."

"Aurora?" Malcolm gazed down at the stunning girl holding on to him for dear life. The artfully curled hair, much like Tamsin's, streamed over her shoulders and was festooned with ribbons. The cut and style of her dress rivaled anything Malcolm had seen on the Continent. His youngest sister was a vision. When last he'd seen Aurora, she'd been digging out the last of the carrots from the hard ground of Dunnings with grim resignation.

"What do you think?" She twirled about before him. "Hester and I needed a walk in the park." She leaned forward. "Doesn't care for London. Misses her chickens. Much like Jordan and his pigs." At his look of confusion, she nodded to the copper-haired woman who had followed in her wake. "Hester. Drew's wife."

Malcolm tossed back the rest of his whiskey and held out the glass for Jordan to refill. After a battle or fight, there was a period when you were glad you'd survived. That's what today felt like for Malcolm. The struggle for the survival of the Sinclairs had lasted more than a decade, but now it was finally over. He looked out over the room, filled with utter joy that his family was whole. Content. No longer living in reduced circumstances.

He slid into a chair and stared at the cart laden with tarts, biscuits, scones, and an assortment of small sandwiches that Holly had wheeled in, and quickly filled a plate, trying not to think of Alyss guarding her virtue and the lone chicken leg.

Aurora chattered away like some crazed parrot, detailing every one of her adventures in London with Miss Maplehurst, who everyone called Aunt Lottie. Her debut would be at the duke's home, which had a magnificent ballroom that could fit half of London. Her gown was a stunning pale blue confection decorated with seed pearls. Ware would be her first dance.

"*He* dances?" Malcolm had a difficult time imagining that large, bearlike creature swirling about Aurora in a graceful manner.

"Splendidly," his sister assured him.

Odessa approached Malcolm about sitting for one of her masks, to which he agreed. He hid his shock at meeting Hester. Drew detested everything about the countryside, but had wed a tart-tongued, red-haired widow who owned a farm in Lincoln-shire. They would stay through Aurora's debut and then return to Blackbird Heath. Drew's wife seemed enormously concerned over her bees.

Dinner was delicious, but not elaborate. Thankfully, because Malcolm wasn't sure he could remember the manners from his childhood. The Sinclairs conversed, joked, hurled insults at each other and generally behaved exactly the way everyone in London expected them to. The only thing that kept Malcolm from complete and absolute contentment at being with his family was Miss Alyss Brooks. What would she make of the Sinclairs?

Later that night after a bath, the haircut and shave would

come tomorrow, Malcolm took Alyss's locket out, turning it over in his hand. He'd have the chain fixed and the locket cleaned, a way of delaying having to return the necklace to her. Because once Malcolm did, he'd have no other excuse to see Alyss again.

And, he thought as he carefully placed the locket on his dresser. He very much wanted one.

CHAPTER TWENTY-ONE

ALYSS SAT QUIETLY in a corner as Lady Hempstead took the podium. She didn't hide, but neither had she engaged in conversation with any of the other ladies involved in this charity. The few acquaintances she'd made while helping orphans declined to speak to Alyss or seek her out. Uncle Richard had warned her, but Alyss had refused to believe anyone would listen to Buckmore.

"Do you wish to leave?" Mrs. Hitchcock sat beside her, back stiff as a poker as she nodded to an acquaintance.

"After Lady Hempstead is finished, we might slip out."

Mrs. Hitchcock nodded. "I think it wise."

The talk about Miss Alyss Brooks had not abated, but neither did it grow. Instead, the gossip of her lover and faked abduction clung to her skirts like a small stain. The sort you hoped no one would notice because it wouldn't wash away no matter what method you tried.

Buckmore had done his job well.

Elizabeth didn't speak to Alyss for nearly an entire week, wandering about the house looking beautiful and melancholy, blaming her father and cousin for the absence of Buckmore. She sent her suitor several notes, all of which Uncle Richard knew about, begging Buckmore to call upon her.

The young baron did not.

Buckmore had finally moved on after his final gambit had

failed. Miss Mary Ellingsworth, the only child of a viscount whose dowry eclipsed Elizabeth's, was the new object of his affections. Miss Ellingsworth also possessed all the intelligence of a pebble. Buckmore would have his heiress and it would not be Elizabeth. That was all that mattered.

Alyss and Uncle Richard breathed a sigh of relief.

Elizabeth remained heartbroken for several days before finally admitting that Alyss had been right. Buckmore couldn't possibly have loved her if he was nearly engaged to Miss Ellingsworth.

"I cannot believe the dowager duchess has lowered herself to associate with that family. Bad enough Ware. How could you possibly attend?"

The scathing tone came from a woman seated in front of Alyss dressed in yellow with an enormous feather protruding from the small hat perched on her head.

"I was invited." The matron, plump and soft, covered in rose satin answered. "And I have no desire to make an enemy of Her Grace as you have. Most of the *ton* was there. Lady Aurora's first dance was with the Duke of Ware. She's a lovely thing, no matter that ridiculous moniker you've bestowed on her family."

"Lovely? She'll end up a wanton like her mother. Perhaps she'll even become an actress."

Alyss leaned forward. There was something about the conversation that made her think of Sinclair, something she'd avoided doing for the last fortnight. Impossible, of course. The moment she closed her eyes at night, Alyss saw him. Green eyes glowing with desire for her, taking her before the fire at Buckmore's cottage.

Knowing he would ruin her life.

"Why would she? Goodness, the Sinclairs will soon be the wealthiest among us."

Alyss's chin snapped up. Her heart beat harder in her chest. *Sinclair.* He'd said his mother had been an actress.

"Were they all there?" The woman in yellow spoke again,

words dripping with disdain. "I wonder that the dowager duchess allows such mongrels in her home."

"Yes. Tamsin Sinclair, of course, since she is the Duchess of Ware now."

The other woman made a sour sound. "I cannot believe the dowager duchess approved her son's marriage to that woman. Especially after breaking the nose of Lord Sokesby at Gunter's. Sokesby must be rolling in his grave that his brother married the woman responsible for such a scandal."

You remind me of my sister. She possesses a vicious right hook.

Alyss's stomach pitched, refusing to settle. Hadn't she suspected Sinclair's family was known in London?

Mrs. Hitchcock leaned over. "Alyss, are you well?"

"Perfectly fine."

"Mr. Andrew Sinclair is wed now and owns an estate in Lincolnshire. I'm told he has entered a business venture with Viscount Worthington's brother."

"He'll rob him and any investors blind," the lady in yellow sniped.

"Lord Emerson and Lady Emerson were in attendance."

"You mean the former Odessa Whitehall. Despicable that she is even permitted out in polite society when her father has fleeced half of London. What about the other? The twin?"

Alyss went completely still.

"I still recall him pummeling my dear Percival when they were children. Horrid, wretched savage. I helped my nephew force him into the military, hoping he'd disappear in some foreign land."

"He was there." The plump lady trilled. "Captain Malcolm Sinclair, though he declines to use the title. Handsome devil. Whatever else you may say about the Sinclairs, Lady Longwood, they are all quite pleasant to look upon."

Alyss sucked in a lungful of air.

Captain Malcolm Sinclair.

Who has a sister that throws a punch. Mother was an actress.

A twin brother.

Not a mercenary. Or a criminal. But the brother of an earl.

Her mind reeled with a dozen different scenarios. Namely why a gentleman such as Malcolm Sinclair was going about kidnapping young ladies for Lord Buckmore. Or being a mercenary.

"I think we should leave, Alyss." Mrs. Hitchcock appeared quite stricken. "You aren't well." She stood and took Alyss's arm, lifted her chin and started moving towards the back of the room. "Don't make eye contact. My goodness. It is worse than I thought."

Alyss looked at her, not understanding how Mrs. Hitchcock could possibly know about Malcolm Sinclair. Then she realized that her companion's manner wasn't due to the gossip she'd overheard about Sinclair.

An entire group of ladies averted their gazes as Alyss walked past. One turned to sniff as if she were a pile of refuse.

Brooks should turn her out.

Anger flooded Alyss's entire body at the loud whisper, one meant to be heard. Her jaw tightened. She stared straight ahead, keeping her posture perfect and her steps unhurried. If she was to become a pariah, she would be a stoic one.

Buckmore had done this to her. But not without help.

A thousand different thoughts, all terrible, flitted through her mind as Mrs. Hitchcock dragged her out in the middle of Lady Hempstead's pretty speech about orphans. No wonder he didn't want Alyss going to the authorities, though it wouldn't matter if she did. No one would believe a former army captain, the brother of an earl and related to a duke would be interested in kidnapping sour Alyss Brooks.

Buckmore and his petty revenge. Sinclair had likely been part of all of it.

A painful sob caught in her throat.

"I think," Mrs. Hitchcock squeezed Alyss's arm. "That the time has come to entertain the proposal Mr. Clinton has put forth to Mr. Brooks. Today has proven to me that the damage has been done. Perhaps we can say that your mysterious lover was Mr. Clinton. Give the entire affair a romantic spin." She nodded. "Yes, I think we could make that work."

"Mr. Clinton?" He of the enormous quivering mustache that dripped crumbs. "But I don't want to wed him."

Mrs. Hitchcock turned to face her. "I'm not sure you have a choice, Alyss. Do you not understand that not one lady inside cared to converse with you? No one greeted us. You were looked at as if you were a common trollop." Her hand fluttered to her throat. "Most distressing."

Alyss's head swam about, near dizzy with all she'd learned. "But Buckmore—"

"It doesn't matter." Mrs. Hitchcock gave her a not so gentle shake as they approached the Brooks carriage. "I believe you, Alyss, as does your uncle. But society is not kind to women. A mere whisper of misconduct and your reputation becomes tattered. It isn't fair."

She sucked in a breath. "I can go away. I can—"

"I think Mr. Clinton," Mrs. Hitchcock kept her voice low as they were ushered inside the privacy of the carriage. "Will provide you a good, comfortable life. Companionship. The gossip will fade once you are wed. As it stands now, you can no longer be seen with Elizabeth, else you will ruin her chances at a good marriage."

Alyss bit her lip. "Is it really so bad as all that?" She cursed Buckmore. But the pain in her heart belonged solely to Malcolm Sinclair.

"Yes, dear." Mrs. Hitchcock drummed her fingers along the window. "It is."

CHAPTER TWENTY-TWO

"MR. CLINTON WASN'T pleased you didn't receive him yesterday. Or the day before." Elizabeth nudged Alyss in the ribs. "Mrs. Hitchcock and I were forced to entertain him until he finally departed. Though I think she rather enjoys playing chaperone, having had no children of her own."

"I hardly need a chaperone at my age." Alyss twirled her new parasol, admiring the gentle flutter of the blue ribbons adorning the top. "And his far too large mustache. Did you enjoy that as well?"

Elizabeth giggled. "The ends got into his tea. A drop caught on his collar."

"Much like a dog slurping at a water bowl."

"Oh, Alyss. You're awful. He's to be your husband." Elizabeth tilted her head. "You must find something about him to like."

She took a deep breath of chilly air, filling her lungs, before releasing it slowly. "Yes, but I didn't agree to the mustache. Only Clinton."

Alyss didn't really want to wed Clinton, but she wanted to cause harm to her family even less.

Her chest squeezed tightly, threatening to steal her breath. The anger towards Sinclair rarely abated, and when it did, the spot was filled with the most horrible longing for him. As if by simply pulling Alyss into his arms, this entire mess would go away.

A mess of his making. And Buckmore's.

Alyss found herself so desolate at times, she kept to the privacy of her room, often just to lay on her bed and stare at nothing for hours. Her usual resilience seemed to have deserted her. She couldn't summon an ounce of indignation.

At least she and Elizabeth were once more on good terms and Buckmore had ceased his pursuit. Elizabeth's affection for the young baron faded dramatically after his defection to another young lady. In the last week alone, Alyss's cousin had mentioned at least three other gentlemen she found rather fetching.

So much for true love.

Better to live without it. And Mr. Clinton.

The prospect of an unwanted marriage loomed before her bigger than that giant caterpillar lining Mr. Clinton's upper lip. How ironic this awful situation had become. Alyss had saved Elizabeth but condemned herself.

After leaving the charity tea with Mrs. Hitchcock, Alyss had been forced to acknowledge that while she'd been right, it had not been wise to chase down Buckmore. The only saving grace in her future marriage to Clinton was that Uncle Richard had agreed to a lengthy courtship so that Alyss might know him better.

In reality, she hoped their betrothal would magically come to an end.

When word of Clinton's courtship of Alyss made its way to society, the speculation was now that he had been Alyss's mysterious lover.

Ugh.

The very thought of Clinton touching her as Sinclair had made the eggs she'd eaten for breakfast swim about in her stomach.

"Oh. There's Mr. Rawlings." Elizabeth's wistful voice broke into Alyss's unwelcome thoughts. Her cousin immediately smoothed her skirts and adjusted her bonnet. She pinched her cheeks. "I confess, I didn't realize he rode so early."

Alyss gave her a sideways glance. "What a happy coincidence."

Elizabeth had been introduced to the young, well-connected barrister at a small gathering held at Lady Curchon's home only last week. Alyss had not attended. Lady Curchon made a point of insisting her presence was not required.

The eggs slid about once more.

Uncle Richard and Mrs. Hitchcock bowed to her wishes. Alyss and her tattered skirts were not required at any of the lavish events Elizabeth attended. Difficult to announce yourself as a young lady's chaperone when everyone in London assumed you'd faked a kidnapping so you could run off with your lover. Who everyone now assumed was Clinton.

Good grief.

Alyss's fingers tightened on the handle of her parasol, wishing Buckmore was present so she could hit him with it. Perhaps take out an eye. Surely, he didn't require both.

A handsome gentleman rode atop a splendid bay gelding in their direction, smiling as he caught sight of Elizabeth. "Miss Brooks." Rawlings smoothly dismounted and strode in their direction.

"Mr. Rawlings," Elizabeth greeted him politely. "How lovely to see you. May I present my cousin, Miss Alyss Brooks."

Rawlings bowed. "Miss Brooks."

If the young barrister knew of Alyss's predicament, or the gossip surrounding her, he gave no indication. His interest rested solely on Elizabeth.

According to Mrs. Hitchcock, Rawlings had his own wealth, left to him by his maternal grandmother and was in no danger of impoverishment or wanting Elizabeth for her dowry. He was polite. Highly intelligent. Attractive. But most importantly, Alyss observed, Rawlings looked at Elizabeth as if she held the world in her hands. He had no intent to deceive or use her for his own purposes.

Alyss pressed a palm to her stomach. She really must ask that the eggs be more well done.

"I should like to take a look at the ducks." Alyss pointed to a small pond a short distance away. "Elizabeth doesn't care for ducks, Mr. Rawlings, I trust you can keep her company for a short time?"

"Of course, Miss Brooks."

She wandered in the direction of the pond, uncaring whether there were ducks or not. Rawlings and Elizabeth were in clear view, though she sensed Rawlings too much of a gentleman to attempt liberties.

Not at all like Malcolm Sinclair.

Alyss had done some poking about into the Earl of Emerson and his family. The Sinclairs were riddled with scandal. Their mother had been an actress and then their father's mistress before becoming Lady Emerson. There had been an elder half-brother, Bentley, who was the nephew of Lady Longwood, which explained her dislike. After the death of their father, Malcolm and his siblings had been banished by their brother from London. An estate in Northumberland, which explained Sinclair's way of speaking if nothing else. Lady Emerson had died there.

I couldn't save my mother either.

The worst part was that the Sinclair family was obnoxiously wealthy. Coal being the source. Malcolm hadn't even needed the money Buckmore offered to kidnap Elizabeth. Yes, they'd had a falling out when Elizabeth wasn't in the carriage, but perhaps Malcolm offered to make it up to his friend by ruining Alyss.

None of it made sense. Nor did it matter. Alyss was still destined to wed Clinton.

She whacked at the tall grass at the edges of the path with her parasol wishing something, anything, would happen so she didn't have to wed Clinton and his mustache. A plague, perhaps. Or Clinton would suddenly fall in love with another woman and jilt Alyss. Anything to keep her from having to marry him to salvage her reputation. A reputation no one in society should ever care about. Alyss was no one. Yet she was no deemed no longer acceptable.

Because Buckmore was a *scurrilous* mongrel.

In her darkest hours, Alyss had a mind to march over to Emerson House and ask for an audience with Lord Emerson. Perhaps he'd like to know what his brother was doing in his spare time. Kidnapping. Stealing horses. Ruining young ladies. Malcolm was a gentleman or at least, his birth deemed him one. He'd feel honor-bound to wed her even if he'd only ruined her to please Buckmore. She'd be saved from the hideous mustache of Clinton.

Alyss looked out over the pond, admiring the way the grass moved about with the breeze.

I don't want him like that.

She didn't want him at all.

Oh, that's a beautiful lie.

Alyss was dangerously close to becoming her mother. The thought terrified her. To have affection for another control her every action. At least with Clinton, her emotions would stay safe. Sealed up. No chance of—

Writhing, naked bodies. His hand holding her in place while he quite thoroughly dominated her and—

A puff of air passed between Alyss's lips. Her fingers trembled on the parasol.

Whenever Mr. Clinton called upon her and took her hand, the anger towards Malcolm Sinclair was so fierce Alyss thought she might explode from the force of it. She detested Buckmore much more, but at least he hadn't bedded her. Hadn't made her feel—

Alyss resolutely pushed that tendril of emotion away. It would not serve her well in the future.

Glancing out over the park, taking in the mist lingering close to the ground as the sunlight tried to dispel it. The way the wet grass sparkled as if lit with brilliants. Her cousin remained in view, a proper distance from Rawlings. The handsome solicitor was nodding at Elizabeth, his features soft and full of tempered adoration. Nothing untoward was happening between them.

Alyss snorted. As if she had any right to judge impropriety.

The crunch of boots on the gravel of the path met her ears. A gentleman approached from the opposite direction, out for an early morning stroll. Alyss's gaze stayed firmly fixed on the ducks floating about the pond. She had no desire to engage in polite acknowledgement or God forbid, conversation. Not when she felt so raw and torn.

"Alyss. I didn't know you even cared for ducks." Sinclair's low rumble floated to her on the breeze. "Keep the parasol pointed to the ground if you don't mind. I don't care to lose an eye before breakfast."

Alyss's skin prickled most deliciously. Gloriously, even. Sparking along her form as if she'd been struck by a bolt of lightning. She fought for composure though her heart screamed at Alyss to go to him.

Remember, he's in league with Buckmore.

Ah, yes. Her heart stopped its shouting in an instant, chastised and wounded. Alyss instead focused on the two young ladies she and Elizabeth had encountered earlier in the park. No eye contact. Muted whispers which ended on an ugly giggle. Faces averted so that they wouldn't have to view the disgrace that was Alyss Brooks.

"Mr. Sinclair." She refused to turn. "Looking for another young lady to kidnap on behalf of Buckmore? Hasn't he told you? Miss Ellingsworth needs no such inducement. Or are you here to provide other services at Buckmore's request as you did at his cottage?"

An annoyed snarl came from him. "Do you honestly believe that Buckmore *paid* me to bed you?"

"Honesty. What a strange concept."

"Alyss—

"I should stab you with my parasol." She commanded her legs to remain steady. "Go away. I didn't report you." She focused on a family of ducks making their way across the pond. "No one would believe me anyway. Buckmore has made sure his nefarious deeds, and yours, will never come to light. According to the gossip he's spread, I planned my own abduction so that no one would guess I was trysting with my lover in Gerryhill."

He took hold of her arm and she jerked away. "Can you not at least look at me while you hurl your accusations?"

Her answer was to whack him in the leg with the parasol. "Thanks to you, my reputation is in tatters."

"I warned you about waving this around." He grabbed hold of the parasol. "I've no idea what you're talking about. I'm not part of society. Nor do I listen to gossip."

"I think you mean the *Deadly Sins* aren't welcome in society, *Captain Malcolm Sinclair*." She tried to free her parasol from his grasp, finally turning to look at him. "And I suppose you don't listen to gossip since so much of it is about your family."

Gone was the thick tangle of beard. Only a tidy line of hair along his jaw and neatly trimmed mustache remained. Nothing at all like Clinton's ridiculous, overblown affair. Hair neatly trimmed, dark strands no longer trailing over the breadth of his shoulders, but still of a length that it curled around his ears. Alyss could see clearly now, the stark, handsome slashes of cheek and strong jaw. Only the bump in his nose remained. And the eyes. A shocking shade of summer grass that nearly glowed in the morning light. Had she not known better, Alyss would never have guessed that this was her abductor, or the man who'd taken her virtue at Gerryhill.

Malcolm Sinclair was quite simply, *magnificent*.

Struck near speechless by his appearance, Alyss thought herself more a fool than ever. Malcolm was far too attractive to have ever chosen to bed the sharp-tongued Alyss Brooks of his own free will. What man that looked like him could possibly desire *her*? Maybe it was a wager between he and Buckmore. Or more likely, he'd owed Buckmore a debt because there was no other reason—

"What did he promise you?" She bit out, horrified. "To destroy me?"

The green eyes hardened, like cold bits of emerald. "Your accusations are insulting."

"But still true, aren't they? she choked. "You don't even deny it." Pain leeched into her heart, an organ she should have better protected. "Had I known—what you really were, I would never have allowed—" A vision of his dark head between her thighs forced her eyes away from him.

"Are you angry because I'm *not* a criminal Alyss?" he said in disbelief. "I was once a mercenary, if that salvages some of your pride. Or makes it that much easier to dismiss me."

"Blackguard." She snapped her wrist and the parasol hit him in the shin.

"You realize that doesn't hurt, don't you? He wrapped an arm around her waist, tugging Alyss in his direction, while she struggled to regain her footing, sparing a glance in the direction of Rawlings and Elizabeth.

"She's very beautiful, isn't she?" Alyss cringed hating the envious note to her words, taking the opportunity to poke him in the thigh with her parasol. "Now you see why I thought you blind for mistaking us."

Malcolm took hold of the parasol with a pointed look. "She resembles a doll my sister once had made of porcelain. I'd break her if I so much as took her hand. Unlike you, my vicious fairy."

Her eyes narrowed, breath halting in her lungs. "Stop calling me names. It does nothing to improve the situation. Release me, this instant. I cannot afford to have my reputation ruined further. You've no idea what Buckmore and you have cost me."

Confusion flickered across his features. "You are determined that this conversation have nothing but sharp edges. Had you a blade, you'd slice at me. Listen to me for a moment. Please."

Alyss stomped on his foot.

Malcolm cursed and grabbed her with both arms, pulling Alyss behind a tree, her back set securely against his chest. She fumed and sputtered, punching out with her fists because he'd taken her parasol.

"Go on, then," she hissed. "Tell me more of your lies. Was I some sort of gentleman's agreement?"

"What—" he said in disbelief. "Your claims become more outlandish with every second. I wasn't sure—what situation I would face when I arrived in London in regards to my family. What their circumstances might be. And you were hell-bent on reporting me to the authorities."

"Well, you made very sure that I could not. Three times. You needn't have bothered. No one would believe the brother of an earl—"

"Four." Malcolm interrupted and pulled his arm tight, forcing the air from her lungs. "Putting my mouth on you counts."

Alyss drew in a shaky breath.

"The idea that you continue to assume Buckmore paid me to tup you is not only insulting, but untrue," he purred along the curve of her ear. "Do not say it again."

Alyss kicked him in the shin, the only part of his body she could reach.

His nose pressed along her neck and inhaled. A low, soft sound came from him. "I am not in league with Buckmore."

She arched back, body humming and sighing into his. The painful ache in Alyss's chest was only for him. Which made her bloody furious. She flailed and kicked, stopping only when he cupped her mound through the layers of petticoats and her dress, the heel of his hand pressing at exactly the right spot.

A tiny sob came from Alyss. A surrender to him and his touch.

"I missed you, vicious fairy," the words were rough. He bent slightly, taking up her skirts, slowly drawing the fabric up her legs. "Shall I demonstrate how much you missed me?"

"You—"

Malcolm placed a palm over her mouth. "You're unreasonably loud, Alyss. Not that I mind. But we are in public. Yet you need convincing, I think."

A soft touch plucked at her stockings stroking along her legs, close to the place waiting between her thighs. This was what she'd dreamt of since leaving Gerryhill. Malcolm touching her. His hands and mouth on her naked flesh. She moaned, lips pressing against his palm.

"Wicked thing."

She caught a glimpse of Elizabeth and Rawlings through the bushes. They were still walking along the path, oblivious to the fact that Alyss was about to be pleasured. She whimpered, pushing her hips forward, shocked at her brazen behavior.

His big, blunt fingers found her flesh, already damp and waiting for his touch. Malcolm drew out the most blissful sensations with each brush of his fingers. "Do you think Buckmore put me up to this Alyss? Do you?"

She couldn't form a coherent thought, not with the gentle caress of his fingers, driving mindless bits of pleasure into her.

Malcolm removed his hand from her mouth, but Alyss declined to say a word. She wanted nothing to ruin this unexpected moment. Not her anger nor her ugly suspicions. When she wed Clinton, this would be all Alyss had. A handful of memories.

Sinclair nipped at her ear, pressing her back more fully against his chest.

The hard length of him pressed into her backside. Good lord, would he lift her skirts and take her against this tree?

Yes. Please.

A moan came from Alyss as he sunk his fingers inside her, stroking the tiny nub hidden in her folds. She was wet and pliable in his arms, like warm honey. It had taken so little effort for Malcolm to arouse her. Merely the brush of his fingers. Each caress sent her further into pleasure, forming a sharp peak, one Alyss longed to topple over.

"I'm going to scream," her voice hitched. "I won't be able to stop it."

"Oh, Alyss." Malcolm breathed, before covering her mouth with his own, swallowing down her cry as she found her release at his hands. Her body jerked in his arms, toes curling inside her half-boots. He held her tight the entire time, claiming every sound she made, lips firmly fixed over hers until nothing was left. Alyss kept her eyes closed, not wanting the passion and comfort she found in his arms to end.

"Alyss!" Elizabeth's panicked voice carried over the grass.

She blinked, glanced down at her splayed legs with his hand fixed between her thighs. Her cousin was coming up the hill and would soon see Alyss with her skirts hitched nearly to her waist, panting like some wild animal in heat—with Malcolm Sinclair.

Alyss took a large gulp of air, horrified and unbelievably, *still aroused*. "Release me. Immediately," she hissed.

Malcolm held her a moment longer, pressing a kiss to her neck. "There are things we should discuss, Alyss."

Alyss grunted and pushed away from him. Her legs were trembling. Body still throbbing. She could smell her own scent on his fingers. Picking up the discarded parasol, she twisted, hitting him on the shoulder. "I'll be there in a moment," she yelled back at her cousin, hitting Sinclair once more for good measure. "I've caught my skirts on a bush."

"I didn't know that Buckmore has spread lies about you, if I had—" Sinclair looked away.

He looked so guilty; Alyss wanted to hit him again. "I'm to be married," she blurted out angrily. "I don't want to hear any more of your paltry excuses," she snapped. "Do not seek me out again. Nor remind me of our association."

He flinched back from her, eyes going flat and cold, but not quick enough to hide what looked like regret. "Such claws and teeth," his voice was rough. "As you wish, Alyss." Malcolm grabbed her hand, forcing something into her palm as Elizabeth and Rawlings climbed up the hill towards them.

Alyss smoothed down her skirts before stepping out from behind the tree and bushes, stooping to pick up the parasol. "I'm right here. Goodness, no need for concern. I was looking at the pond and my skirts snagged on a bush. There was a tiny family of ducks." She pretended to look out over the water. "Did you see them?"

More importantly, had Elizabeth seen Sinclair looming over Alyss? Touching her? Hopefully he'd disappeared at catching sight of her cousin. Alyss could ill afford any more conjecture about her morals or lack of them.

"Are you alone?" Elizabeth caught up to her with Mr. Rawlings just behind. "I thought I saw you speaking to a gentleman." She leaned to the side, peering into the wooded area behind Alyss.

Her heart skipped about, waiting for Elizabeth to catch sight of Malcolm. Her hand clasped tighter on what lay in her palm. Alyss knew the shape as well as she knew her own name.

Her mother's locket.

She turned slightly, scanning the line of trees for his broad form, but Malcolm was gone. Driven away by Alyss and her ugly, awful words.

The locket was warm in her hand. Searing her with the knowledge that the things she'd said to Malcolm. Too late now, to take any of it back.

"Well, yes. A lovely gentleman," she forced a smile to her lips.

"Oh, I—" Elizabeth said in a confused tone. "He looked a little like—"

"Like who?" Alyss took her cousin's arm, turning back to Rawlings.

"The man who had Buckmore abduct you. I mean me," she whispered with a wave of her hand. "What I meant to say—"

"Is you are in need of spectacles," Alyss said, crisply, attempting to compose herself. Her legs were unsteady, as if the ground below her was moving beneath her feet. "The kind gentleman you glimpsed found my locket in the grass and returned it to me. The clasp must have broken without my noticing." Alyss opened her hand to show Elizabeth the necklace. "You know how devastated I would be to lose it." Moisture gathered in her eyes as she studied her most prized possession. He had ridden all the way back to Gerryhill and hunted down Elrood to find the locket.

All for Alyss.

Definitely the actions of a man who had only tupped her to please Buckmore. She'd never even allowed him to explain. Because Alyss always had to be right.

Anguish struck her and she stumbled.

Elizabeth's brows drew together. "I don't recall you wearing your locket today—"

"Nonsense. I rarely take it off," Alyss replied. "The clasp broke and fell into the grass as I watched the ducks."

Mr. Rawlings had retreated back down the hill ahead of them and now stood beside his horse, peering in the direction of the woods. He bowed to Elizabeth and Alyss as they approached.

Elizabeth waved at him with a smile. "Mr. Rawlings grew concerned. I had to stop him from storming up the hill to defend your honor."

"My honor was never in question," Alyss assured her.

"What was his name?" she said lightly. "You should send him a note, thanking him for his assistance. It would be the polite thing to do."

"He did not introduce himself," Alyss murmured wishing her cousin would just let the matter rest. She brought out her list, the one which declared Malcolm Sinclair a liar. No better than Buckmore. But her indignation was gone, banished by the feel of his mouth on hers and the locket in her hand.

"Hmm. Well, that is unfortunate," Elizabeth said quietly. "I should have liked to meet him."

⟫⟫⟫⟩⟨⟨⟨⟪

MALCOLM STAYED WELL hidden in the thick trees bordering the pond as he watched Alyss walk away. She glanced behind her, searching for him a perplexed look on her delicate, sharp features before disappearing down the hill with her cousin.

Once they'd disappeared, he walked out of the wooded area to a spot further down the path to retrieve his horse. A hollowness took up residence inside him.

Married. Alyss was going to wed. Because of Buckmore.

Because of me.

Guilt assailed him. He'd ruined her life, and she rightfully blamed him. Malcolm had known well before the carriage reached Gerryhill that the woman he'd taken wasn't Elizabeth Brooks. He should have turned the bloody carriage around. But—

A mistake. Today's meeting with Alyss had been a mistake. Malcolm had only meant to give Alyss the locket, not pounce on her, demanding her surrender. He hadn't meant to leave the park with the scent of her pleasure on his fingers.

That was the problem with Miss Alyss Brooks. She blinded Malcolm to everything else. Even the fact that Buckmore meant to destroy her so completely that she was forced to marry some unknown gentleman that Malcolm already wanted to strangle.

He reached his horse, pressing his fingers into the leather of the saddle, trying to clear his head that Alyss's soft sounds and sharp words would now belong to someone else.

Climbing into the saddle, he turned towards the path leading out of the park. Malcolm didn't listen to gossip as a rule and thus had heard nothing of Alyss and the scandal Buckmore created. Malcolm had avoided most of London society since his return, save those present at Aurora's debut. He still remembered how the *ton* had treated his mother.

Buckmore had ensured Alyss would receive the same treatment. And Malcolm hadn't known. Well, he did now. Alyss may not want him, but that wouldn't stop Malcolm from protecting her.

It was past time to pay a visit to Buckmore and remind that pampered little prick of his manners.

CHAPTER TWENTY-THREE

A LYSS'S FINGERS TREMBLED on the spine of the book before she deftly plucked it from the shelf. She'd spent the entire ride home from the park with Elizabeth trying to convince herself she was right about Malcolm. He was in league with Buckmore. He'd tupped her out of amusement. Or possibly Buckmore made him a wager. No matter that she'd seen Malcolm's dislike of Buckmore firsthand. Or that Malcolm denied his association with the young lord. Besides, so what if he truly felt something for her, it would be bound to end in disaster. Love wasn't part of her future. Couldn't be. She'd accepted that long ago.

Alyss was *certain* she was right.

She sat the book down and reached up to her throat where the locket was once more secured. He'd had it cleaned. She could clearly see the words her father had inscribed so long ago on the back. The chain was new. Her fingers trembled as she let the locket once more fall to lay against her chest.

Would it be so terrible to be wrong? In this instance?

Hope had bloomed in Alyss after that meeting in the park, a timid, fragile thing. Malcolm would appear and demand to see her. Demand she listen to him. Foolish, given how awful Alyss had been.

Alyss took a sharp breath, pressing a hand over her still flat belly.

Neither Malcolm nor her courses appeared to Alyss over the

following week, only nausea after breakfast every day. The grim reality was that Malcolm wasn't going to appear because Alyss, determined to be right, had made sure he wouldn't.

And now there was *no* choice in her marrying Mr. Clinton and his terrible mustache.

A sob threatened to crawl up her throat and she resolutely pushed it away. This was no time to falter. Her spine was made of steel. Forged in that bloody desert when Alyss was a child. She was nothing if not resilient. The blame for her current circumstances, was hers. Confronting Buckmore had not been wise, but Alyss found she couldn't regret doing so.

She did consider sending Malcolm a note, but what would she say? Apologize, then immediately ask he be honorable? How ridiculous. He hadn't tried to see her since the day in the park.

"It doesn't matter," she whispered, allowing a wave of sadness to engulf her.

"What doesn't?" Elizabeth bounced into the drawing room, a bright smile on her face.

"Whether I finish this book or not," Alyss said smoothly. "You're quite happy. Has something happened with Mr. Rawlings?" Elizabeth mentioned the handsome barrister more often than not. Her cousin was often flighty in her affections, but the way she spoke of Mr. Rawlings was different.

"After he called yesterday, Mr. Rawlings spoke to Papa in private. He wishes to court me." Elizabeth rolled back and forth on her feet. "I am over the moon, Alyss. He's quite wonderful."

"I agree." Alyss smiled back, masking her own unhappiness. Rawlings *was* wonderful. Steady. Mature. He would be a good match for her cousin.

"You approve of him?"

"Wholeheartedly," Alyss assured her. Rawlings was nothing like Buckmore.

That scurrilous cur was officially betrothed to Miss Ellingsworth. He was now her problem and that of her father, the viscount. Which might account for why the gossip about Alyss had suddenly and abruptly halted. Not only that, but when she'd spied Buckmore at the bookseller's, on the lone occasion she'd left the house besides walking in the park, he had studiously avoided Alyss. Not a hint of mockery touched his lips. He hadn't even glared at her.

Not even Buckmore thought her of import any longer.

"Alyss, you are very pale. Is your stomach still distressed? You barely ate anything at breakfast." Elizabeth's face was full of concern.

No, I'm not well. Alyss wanted to scream. *I've broken my own heart, shattered it into a thousand tiny bits and I must wed a man who I find repulsive. And I find myself with child after having driven away the father, the man I—*

Alyss didn't dare think more. Couldn't allow herself to even whisper the word. She'd spent her entire life *avoiding* romantic entanglements and affection choosing to remain unwed.

The irony was suffocating.

"I'm fine, Elizabeth. This morning I had a most pleasant carriage ride with Mr. Clinton through the park." She'd gazed out at the trees the entire time, looking for Malcolm, barely listening to Mr. Clinton drone on about the details of their small wedding ceremony which would take place at the Brooks home tomorrow at approximately one o'clock.

Another wave of nausea had Alyss gripping the arm of the chair.

Her lack of interest in their upcoming nuptials was taken by Mr. Clinton as a sign Alyss preferred he take liberties with her person during their carriage ride. Shocked to be accosted by his terrible mustache, she had to swat him with her parasol. Not only did she dissuade him, but the parasol knocked off the bit of egg dangling from one corner of his mouth, trapped in all that waxed hair.

Mr. Clinton was barely deterred. He had the audacity to discreetly squeeze her bottom upon his departure.

Elizabeth perched on the edge of the settee. "The gossip has died down. In a few months, no one will remember the tiny scandal you were embroiled in. "You do not have to wed Mr. Clinton. There is still time to call off the marriage."

"I have no intention of doing so."

Her cousin clasped her hands. "Mr. Clinton is horrid," Elizabeth stated bluntly. "You don't like him. Why would you go forward with wedding him? More importantly, how on earth are you supposed to," she lowered her voice. "Do your marital duties?"

"I'll think of England. And what do you know of such things?"

"Enough that you won't enjoy yourself with Mr. Clinton."

Alyss pursed her lips. "Elizabeth," she chastised. "I have committed myself to wedding Mr. Clinton. A vicar has been summoned. I've purchased a new dress." She plucked at her skirts. "The trouble with Buckmore only made me realize Mr. Clinton's positive attributes. I've grown accustomed to him."

That was the kindest thing Alyss could say about her future husband. She did not look forward to sharing a bed with him, but now she must.

"What about the gentleman in the park?" Elizabeth gave her a pointed look. "Does he know you're going to wed Mr. Clinton for no good reason?"

Alyss pretended great shock at the mention of Malcolm. Elizabeth had seen them together, after all. "You mean the gentleman who found my locket in the grass? Why, I barely recall what he looks like, let alone his name. Which he did not give me."

"Odd. You were standing so close. I thought surely he might have introduced himself." Elizabeth leaned in. "Or possibly you are already acquainted. There a great deal of familiarity between you."

She inhaled slowly. "You are quite fanciful. He merely returned my locket. Nothing more. I thanked him and he went on his way."

"Hmm." Her cousin tapped one finger on her chin. "Yes, I suppose you did thank him. *Profusely*. Should I go on? I am not in need of spectacles, Alyss."

Alyss went perfectly still, warmth creeping up her cheeks. This was rather horrifying. "You are reading far too many romantic novels, I think. Your imagination—"

Elizabeth threw up her hands before she turned to glare at Alyss. Her eyes were a vibrant, determined blue. And shrewd. Far too shrewd. "I don't know who this mysterious gentleman is, Alyss. But I would venture you like him far better than Mr. Clinton." When Alyss said nothing, Elizabeth continued, "I see you are determined to be right in this as well." She waved her hand and stood. "I suppose we shall all get used to Mr. Clinton."

Those words sent a wave of dread through Alyss.

"I ruined it," she whispered at Elizabeth's back as her cousin sailed from the room. Her fingers were cold, no matter how she buried them in her skirts. Her future was inescapable. Brought on by her own stubbornness.

CHAPTER TWENTY-FOUR

"CAPTAIN SINCLAIR, I'M sorry to interrupt."

Malcolm didn't look up from the pistol he was cleaning. "Just Sinclair or Malcolm, please, Holly." He'd reminded the butler at least a half-dozen times that addressing him as if he were still a soldier wasn't pleasing. Captain Sinclair was part of Malcolm's past, and he didn't wish to revisit that life. His focus needed to remain on the future.

A future lacking the one thing he could not have. Alyss.

Kidnapping was still a consideration, of course. He hadn't ruled it out.

"Apologies, *Mr.* Sinclair." Holly cleared his throat. "There is a young lady asking to see you. At the kitchen door."

Malcolm looked up in confusion. "A lady? To see me?" Staying away from Alyss had been difficult. Knowing she meant to wed another man, excruciating. But had she come to him? The hopeful thump of his heart wanted it to be Alyss.

"She did not give her name, only insisted on speaking with you as soon as possible. She said it was a personal matter of great urgency."

It could be no one else but Alyss.

He set down the pistol and rag. Had she come about Buckmore?

Malcolm's visit to the young lord had come shortly after his encounter with Alyss in the park. The pampered little toad had not been pleased to see Malcolm sitting nonchalantly in his study. Buckmore had just arrived home from an evening out, probably at a brothel since he smelled of cheap perfume and his cravat was untied.

He'd tried to be polite. Honestly. But Buckmore was such a sniveling worm of a man. Alyss was completely correct about his character.

Malcolm had insisted, in no uncertain terms, that Buckmore cease his destruction of Alyss Brooks' reputation, or he'd live to regret his actions.

"Don't tell me you are concerned over plain, sour Alyss Brooks. How touching," Buckmore had sneered. "Perhaps my tale of Gerryhill held much more truth than I first surmised."

Malcolm's response was a fist to Buckmore's left eye.

Alyss was *not* plain. Only sour. But he didn't mind in the least. Malcolm liked tart things.

"I'll report you to the authorities." Buckmore had whined, holding his eye.

"Go ahead, you'll only incriminate yourself, you bloody idiot." Malcolm punched him again, this time in the nose. "My sister is wed to the Duke of Ware as you'll likely recall. Something you failed to mention to me in Calais. Any accusation you make will disappear under his direction." Malcolm paused. "Or that of Lord Curchon, the duke's uncle. No wonder you kept bringing him up."

"I didn't want you to run afoul of Curchon. He is close to Mr. Brooks." Blood spurted from Buckmore's nose even as his eye started to swell.

"Wrong answer." Malcolm's next target was Buckmore's jaw. "You also neglected the somewhat important information that my family now owned one of the largest coal deposits in England and was no longer impoverished."

"You wouldn't have taken the job of kidnapping Elizabeth had you known," Buckmore sniffed, holding up his hands before collapsing on the ground at Malcolm's feet. "I yield."

"You've little choice but to yield. Here are how things will go from this point forward. Not another word about Alyss Brooks. In fact, you will quietly recant your version of events. You were foxed. Need spectacles. Angry that she interfered with your courtship of her cousin. I don't care what reason you give. The point being, no more unfavorable talk of Alyss. Or you won't have time to enjoy your good fortune with Miss Ellingsworth."

Holly cleared his throat once more, reminding Malcolm of his presence and dispelling the conversation with Buckmore.

"I'll be along directly," he said. "Ask Mrs. Cherry to provide our guest with tea."

The butler bowed and retreated.

Standing, Malcolm didn't bother with a coat. Alyss had seen him in much less than his shirtsleeves. Did she believe him now? Is that what she had come to say? There was no more gossip, Malcolm had seen to that. Perhaps she would no longer wed this other gentleman.

Unless this man was one she cared for.

A pinch occurred above his chest.

He was now in a position to offer Alyss something more than a slightly tattered ex-mercenary from a notorious, impoverished family. The Sinclairs had more than enough wealth and Malcolm could decide how to spend his time. Make his own future. He'd discussed his plans with Jordan, who agreed. Alyss could be part of this new venture. His partner in all things.

Mrs. Cherry, the Earl of Emerson's cook, stood facing the stairs as Malcolm entered the kitchen. She was chatting away to a young lady who sat across the large kitchen worktable, a cup of steaming tea before her. The lady's back, covered in blue muslin, faced Malcolm.

Slender, gloved hands picked up the tea and took a sip as Mrs. Cherry noted Malcolm's arrival.

"Mr. Sinclair," the cook greeted him.

At least someone listened to his instruction not to address Malcolm by his military rank.

"Miss Brooks and I were just getting acquainted," Mrs. Cherry informed him.

"Thank you, Mrs. Cherry. You can go about your duties."

She nodded politely and left the kitchen. Her footsteps faded as she trotted down the hall to the larder. Close enough to be on hand for propriety's sake, but far enough she wouldn't hear them.

"Alyss."

A pair of blue eyes shone back at him as the young lady turned, a smile transforming her features from outrageously pretty to stunning. But there were no claws or teeth in this woman because she was not Alyss. Malcolm's disappointment was so fierce he had to struggle to hide it.

"I'm not my cousin, Mr. Sinclair." Miss Elizabeth Brooks gave him a direct look. "I will try not to take your disappointment at my appearance to heart."

He carefully composed his features into a polite, confused inquiry. "I don't believe we're acquainted, Miss?"

Her shoulders rose and fell in resignation, though the smile didn't falter. "Really, Mr. Sinclair. Very well, I am Miss Elizabeth Brooks, cousin of Miss Alyss Brooks. As I believe you are well aware given you were hired to abduct me by Lord Buckmore."

Elizabeth Brooks *was* beautiful. He could see why Buckmore had wanted her. But Malcolm's heart didn't beat wildly in his chest at the sight of her in his kitchen. Nor did he have the slightest urge to touch her. Or tup her on the kitchen worktable, something he would have attempted had it been Alyss.

"I'm sorry." He shook his head. "I have no idea what you're referring to Miss Brooks. Abduction? Why we've never even met." Possibly, he'd underestimated Alyss. For all Malcolm knew she'd been so annoyed by being groped in the park she'd sent her cousin to flush him out.

"*Really,* Mr. Sinclair." Elizabeth gave an elegant wave. "I'm quite discreet. I know Lady Mayfield is a notorious gossip and no great friend of the Sinclairs, thus I came round the back. There has been enough undue speculation as of late, don't you think?

You know," she tapped her chin with one gloved finer. "Until recently, I'd forgotten there was *another* Sinclair. Your sister, Lady Aurora, came out, which was news, of course. Lord Emerson's marriage. And then, everyone speaks of Lady Tamsin," her eyes widened. "I mean, the duchess. I confess, I did catch a glimpse of Mr. Andrew Sinclair once at a party I attended. We didn't speak. But you look nothing alike, though Mr. Rawlings claims you are twins."

Malcolm kept his features impassive during her chattering. "None of that explains why you have sought me out, Miss Brooks."

"Goodness." She rolled her eyes. "You are determined to make this difficult. You are nearly as stubborn as Alyss. Lord Buckmore hired you to kidnap me in the park some weeks ago so that I could be compromised and forced to wed him. You took Alyss instead of me. I suppose you confused us though we look nothing alike. I rarely forget a face, or the shape of a person." She peered at him. "Even clean shaven as you are now, I know it was you. Just as I did the other day when Alyss claimed to be looking at the ducks. She doesn't even like ducks, Mr. Sinclair."

"Forgive me, Miss Brooks. But you are mistaken. I've never met your cousin, or Lord Buckmore. Allow me to escort you out." He bowed slightly and waved her forward.

"I am not going to the authorities. I've no reason to." Elizabeth tilted up her chin. "And it is doubtful they would believe me at any rate. Nor did Buckmore send me. I haven't spoken to him since Alyss's return. I must say I am grateful for your lack of attention that day, else that scoundrel might have ruined me. Please put yourself at ease. I'm here about Alyss."

Malcolm turned, feigning great interest in a bowl of apples. Was Alyss ill? Had she been in an accident? As soon as Elizabeth was gone from the kitchen, Malcolm would make careful inquiries. Possibly break into the Brooks home to make sure Alyss was well.

Just the thought of seeing her sent an ache through him.

"Again," he said calmly. "I am not familiar with your cousin, Miss Brooks."

"I see I must speak plainly. I have surmised that since you are the kidnapper hired by Lord Buckmore, you must *also* have been with Alyss at Gerryhill."

Malcolm stared right back at her. Elizabeth wasn't as oblivious to the world as Alyss assumed her to be.

"I'd almost forgotten about Buckmore's cottage. We once picnicked there. Alyss chaperoned." A frown crossed her pretty features. "I do not think she enjoyed herself, though she did have an opportunity to poke Buckmore in the ribs with her parasol for sitting far too close to me."

Knowing Alyss's dislike of Buckmore, it was a wonder he'd survived the outing.

"At any rate," Elizabeth continued. "If the dreadful storm that caught Alyss forced her into Buckmore's cottage, I'm equally certain you sought shelter there as well. There is literally nothing else in Gerryhill. A stable and smithy. Possibly a small shop of some sort. But no inn. I suppose you could have slept in the stables, but I doubt it, not when there was a fully stocked larder and a warm fire just around the corner." Miss Brooks looked entirely too pleased with herself. "You and Alyss were alone together for an entire day and night and that doesn't include you bringing her back to London, as you surely must have done." She leaned forward. "Incredibly gentlemanly of you, by the way, considering the circumstances."

Elizabeth leaned back once more. "Now, you are probably wondering how I knew the kidnapper hired by Buckmore was *you*, Malcolm Sinclair. I recognized you, but I didn't know your name. Mr. Rawlings *did*. He's a barrister of some note." Her cheeks pinked. "And is acquainted with Mr. Patchahoo."

Bloody hell. Patchahoo was the Sinclair family's solicitor.

"Miss Brooks." Malcolm needed to put a stop to this immediately, and send Alyss's far too inquisitive cousin on her way.

"I saw you with Alyss, Mr. Sinclair," she blurted out, as the blush deepened further on her cheeks. "Taking," she cleared her throat. "Liberties. Alyss did not object. In fact, she looked as if she were enjoying herself a great deal."

"Is there a point to this conversation, Miss Brooks?" Malcolm growled.

"Goodness. No wonder you were a kidnapper." She pretended to quiver in fear. "You're very menacing. Alyss *did* look terrified when you had your hands up her skirts," she said, with no small amount of sarcasm, the effect ruined when Elizabeth's entire face turned a shade of plum. "My eyesight is quite good, despite what my cousin thinks."

The kitchen grew silent.

Mrs. Cherry stuck her head out of the larder, took one look at Malcolm's scowling features, and disappeared once more.

"So, as to why I've come today, well that has to do with Alyss. I understand you claim not to be acquainted with my cousin. However, I thought I should tell you that she plans to wed Mr. Edward Clinton today at one o'clock."

Malcolm sucked in a breath. Alyss hadn't been lying. "What's that," he rasped. "Have to do with me?" Married. Today. His chest tightened so abruptly, Malcolm thought he might suffocate.

"Mr. Clinton is suitable enough, I suppose, though he possesses an atrocious mustache. He has admired Alyss for some time, though she has never encouraged his attentions. But my father thought that given Alyss's scandal, or rather the scandal Buckmore created, that she should wed to spare us a great deal of shame. However, Buckmore has since recanted." She gave Malcolm a careful look. "A broken nose and a black eye will do that, I'm told." Accusation gleamed in her eyes.

"Maybe Lord Buckmore was in a brawl of some sort."

"Buckmore?" Elizabeth burst into a fit of giggles. "Good lord, he's terrified of Alyss. I'm not sure what I ever saw in him."

"Again, Miss Brooks—"

"So, in the absence of gossip," she ignored his interruption, "and the need to protect me further because Mr. Rawlings will likely offer for me, Alyss is *still* going to wed Mr. Clinton. She insists upon it though I have tried to dissuade her. The very idea of wedding Clinton is making my cousin ill." Another pointed look skewered Malcolm. "Tossing up her breakfast nearly *every* morning as she faces her future, and drifting about pale and melancholy. I love my cousin and grew concerned. I brought my observations to Mrs. Hitchcock."

"Who the bloody hell is Mrs. Hitchcock?" Alyss was ill. Had been. For weeks.

"A widow who my father—well, that is not important. Alyss does not love Mr. Clinton or even *like* him. I believe her affections are elsewhere." She glared at him. "So what do you suppose her reasoning is?"

"I've no idea," Malcolm snapped back at Elizabeth, furious over what she implied. His mind raced with the knowledge that Alyss, his little fairy, she—

"Still unwilling to admit to your acquaintance with Alyss?" Miss Brooks retied the ribbon of her bonnet and stood, smoothing down her skirts. "I hadn't thought you to be a stupid man, though considering you were involved with Buckmore, perhaps you are. You cannot even put two and two together."

Alyss would have sent for him. *Should* have sent for him. "She told me she never wanted to speak to me again."

"And you believed her?" Elizabeth rolled her eyes.

"She said," Malcolm thundered, "she was wedding another man."

"Yes, but the man is Mr. Clinton." Her lips rolled in disgust. "At one o'clock, Mr. Sinclair. Today. I apologize for the delay in relaying the information, but it took some time for Mr. Rawlings to—"

"I don't care." Indeed, the only thing Malcolm cared for at all was Alyss.

"I suggest you make your interest known before then." She shrugged as if it didn't matter. "Or make her a widow at some point in the future. If you have the courage to do so. Good lord, if you are an example of the type of soldier protecting England, we are all in trouble."

Malcolm gritted his teeth, refusing to acknowledge her goading. She was as bad as Alyss. But brave. Tenacious. Not many young women would have marched into Emerson House to confront him.

"Alyss is fortunate to have you as a cousin, Miss Brooks."

"Indeed, she is." Then with a tilt of her bonnet, Miss Elizabeth Brooks hopped up the stairs and out the kitchen door, without so much as a goodbye.

Malcolm pulled out a chair and looked at the clock above the stove as it struck ten. Not much time. Under no circumstances was he about to allow Alyss to wed this Clinton, especially when he suspected, after Elizabeth's not so subtle hints, that Alyss was with child.

His child.

There was also the small matter that he loved Alyss. Impossible as that seemed. But he did.

After a few moments, Mrs. Cherry ventured back into the kitchen. "I find a slice of pie helps one sort things out, Mr. Sinclair. Will apple do?"

"Apple pie would be most welcome," he assured her, tracing a groove in the table. "But only one slice. There is something urgent I need to do."

CHAPTER TWENTY-FIVE

"THERE ISN'T ANY reason for you to keep wearing a hole in my rug, Elizabeth. What is wrong with you, today? First you disappear for over an hour, and no one can find you, and now you are determined to pace about and not settle."

"You forgot to mention my badgering about the gentleman in the park." Her voice had an oddly wistful sound. "The one that you allowed liberties."

Alyss pursed her lips refusing to acknowledge her cousin's accusations. "Has Rawlings done something?" She watched her cousin. "For the life of me, I can't imagine that he has."

"I went for a carriage ride. Nothing more." Elizabeth glanced at the clock. "I'm prepared," she waved carelessly at her dress. "For the wedding." The last was said with a great deal of dislike.

Yes, but Alyss was not prepared. Her stomach lurched unpleasantly the closer the time drew to one o'clock. She felt as if she might scream. Loudly. Every fiber of her being insisted Alyss stop this nonsense immediately and *run* to Emerson House. Malcolm would do the right thing.

Yes, but—there was the rub.

Would Malcolm want her *only* because of her condition?

That might break Alyss far worse than wedding Clinton.

Her cousin paused, pulled back the drapes, and peered out Alyss's bedroom window which overlooked the street below. "Oh dear. Mr. Clinton has arrived. Early. I had really hoped—"

Alyss closed her eyes. She should ask Elizabeth to pass her the basin hidden beneath her bed. She was going to be ill. "What did you hope?"

"Nothing." Elizabeth shook her head. "The vicar isn't due for another hour. I suppose Mr. Clinton merely wants to enjoy a brandy with Papa before the—proceedings."

The blue silk gown felt sticky against Alyss's skin. Wrong in every way. "I think I'll stay in my room until—will you fetch me when the vicar arrives?" Uncle Richard had arranged for the vicar to perform the brief ceremony making her Mrs. Edward Clinton. There were no guests other than Mrs. Hitchcock.

"I love you Alyss, truly," Elizabeth's tone was quiet. "You are so wise about a great many things, but in this instance, your stubbornness has overridden common sense. I don't know why you would rather wed the detestable Clinton rather than the man you truly care for. The man I suspect you love."

A small cry came from Alyss.

"No matter how complicated or how strange the beginning. How can this possibly be better?"

Alyss didn't look up or answer. What could she say? It most certainly wasn't better. But she'd driven Malcolm away. He no longer wanted her.

Elizabeth strode to the door. "Tell me to send a note for you. *Now*. Immediately and I will do it."

Alyss's fingers curled into her skirts. "A note? For what reason?" And have Malcolm ignore it? What would she even say?

A frustrated breath left Elizabeth. "Oh, Alyss," she said, with a great deal of sadness. "I hope the stubbornness you cling to will bring you peace once wed to Clinton. I fear little else will." Elizabeth opened the door and stepped into the hall. "I'll inform them both you'll be down when the vicar arrives."

Alyss didn't answer, willing the moisture gathering behind her lashes to not become a wealth of tears. She hadn't cried over her situation. Not once. And she couldn't bear to do so now.

Elizabeth knew, really knew, about Malcolm.

There was no other explanation for her cousin's behavior. Which meant Rawlings knew as well. Possibly he'd also seen her behaving like some harlot that day in the park. So much for maintaining her decorum.

Well, you did give your virtue to a mercenary after a botched kidnapping.

A fist pressed against her mouth to stifle the sob coming from her lips.

Sounds from downstairs filtered up to her. The front door opening. The quick steps of Mr. Clinton against the tile as he was invited inside. Uncle Richard's greeting, though he didn't sound nearly as effusive as he had before.

Her uncle had taken Alyss aside last night and gently told her that she need not wed Clinton to salvage her reputation or that of the family. Lord Curchon had even told Uncle Richard over a glass of brandy that no one believed Buckmore's tale any longer. It had seemed outlandish from the beginning and Buckmore had reluctantly admitted to have been drinking. As far as Elizabeth, she was deemed impressionable with a vivid imagination.

Pity Lord Curchon hadn't stepped in immediately upon Alyss's return from Gerryhill, but then she recalled that the Duke of Ware was Lord Curchon's nephew. Ware was wed to Tamsin Sinclair, Malcolm's sister.

Malcolm had silenced Buckmore. Just as he'd gotten back her mother's locket.

All for me.

Alyss had never believed in love at first sight, mainly because her parents claimed to have fallen in love at their first meeting. She'd mocked the idea for years. Love was a manipulation. The evidence of her mother's death was clear.

"I need some air." She said out loud, though she was alone.

Alyss needed to think, *really* think. First, she'd assumed Malcolm didn't want her or would ever bed a woman like Alyss so she'd lashed out at him, refusing to admit to her own feelings. Determined to think him deceitful. Yet he'd vanquished Buckmore on her behalf. Found her locket. Now she'd convinced herself that Malcolm would only want her because of the child she carried. And she was about to wed a detestable man to prove that she was right.

Would you rather be right or wise, Alyss?

"I want to be happy," she breathed out loud.

CHAPTER TWENTY-SIX

MALCOLM WATCHED THE carriage pull up to the Brooks home and a short, red-faced man jump out, smooth back his hair and march up the steps. It wasn't one o'clock yet, but his gut told him that was Clinton.

Older. Bandy legged. Permanent scowl on his features as he climbed the stairs to the Brooks home. Looked like a bulldog.

Malcolm's nose wrinkled. What the bloody hell was Alyss thinking?

Was she even thinking at all? How in the world could Clinton be a better choice than Malcolm? Granted, Clinton's family wasn't notorious. And he hadn't mistakenly kidnapped Alyss. But she really thought to doom herself to sharing intimacies with— Malcolm eyed Clinton again. Not a bulldog. More a *frog*.

Malcolm was going to kidnap Alyss again. This time on purpose. He loved her. There wasn't an alternative because Alyss was being stubborn.

Moving closer to the house, which was thankfully circled by an enormous hedge, Malcolm wedged between the plants and the window so he could look into the drawing room. Taking a quick peek, Malcolm caught sight of Elizabeth. A man he took to be Mr. Brooks, Alyss's uncle. And Clinton. But no sign of Alyss or a vicar, which meant there was still time.

He took out his watch. At least half an hour.

Malcolm hadn't meant to cut the time so close, but he'd had

to collect his thoughts after Elizabeth's visit and determine a plan of action. He had sat in the kitchens while Mrs. Cherry bustled about, and eaten two slices of apple pie while he planned. Malcolm was bloody furious with Alyss. He wanted to shake her senseless. Obviously, she didn't want him to do the honorable thing, which *really* annoyed Malcolm. First, because he wasn't all that honorable. Secondly, how could Alyss think he wouldn't want her? The moment he'd seen her stumbling down the road in Gerryhill, wet and covered in muck, Malcolm had been lost to Alyss Brooks.

It was the second piece of pie that had given Malcolm true clarity.

His fairy was terrified. Of him. Of love. She'd gone to great lengths to concoct various reasons to push him away. Alyss didn't need to tell Malcolm that, he heard it when she spoke of her parents. The disdain for her father.

Bloody stubborn spinster.

Malcolm's original plan had been to knock on the door, bully the Brooks butler and force his way into the drawing room. Ask to speak to Alyss privately. Possibly punch Clinton if he objected. But that would cause quite a ruckus. Kidnapping her made more sense.

He expected Alyss would be difficult and was prepared to subdue her.

The entire lower half of his body tightened.

God, I hope so.

Malcolm moved silently along the side of the house, making sure to keep himself hidden behind the enormous hedge. He would scale the wall surrounding the garden, creep inside and find Alyss's room. Malcolm wasn't sure what he would say, but he'd think of something. Hopefully, they'd argue and end up naked in Alyss's bed. Being caught in a compromising situation would certainly resolve the situation quickly.

Malcolm climbed over the wall, dropping to his feet with a quiet thud. Breaking into a residence wasn't difficult. Buckmore's home, for instance, had been ridiculously easy.

His foot landed next to a cluster of white flowers, struggling to survive in a patch of sunlight.

"Dear God, what are you doing here?"

That crisp, precise tone never failed to stir Malcolm. It was criminal how easily Alyss aroused him with just a sentence.

She was staring at him through a mulberry bush, pitch black eyes wide in shock.

"Inspecting the flowers." Malcolm raised one hand. "Don't scream." No parasol in sight, but a branch or two littered the ground at her feet. "You will not be wedding Clinton. He resembles a frog."

"What—"

"Or the ugliest dog I've ever seen. Frankly, Alyss, it's insulting you would choose to shackle yourself to him rather than me. I caught sight of him, so don't you dare tell me he's perfectly acceptable. You will not marry him. I forbid it."

"You forbid it?" Alyss tilted her chin defiantly, her spine straightening as if a spike were drawn down the back of her gown. "How dare—"

"How dare *you*, Alyss Brooks?" The anger in Malcolm's voice made his meaning clear. Alyss looked lovely and fragile in her wedding finery. A gown she meant to wed that bloody frog in. The heavy, nearly white mass of her hair was piled atop her head, one small curl dangling at her temple. It hurt so much to see her like that. Dressed for another man.

"At least Elizabeth had the bravery to tell me when you could not."

Alyss's bravado crumpled, the determined look on her face shattering. She bit into her bottom lip so hard, Malcolm thought she might draw blood. "I should have told you, but—"

"Yes, you should have." Malcolm snapped. "I'm quite angry with you, Alyss. It might take some time for me not to be. Keeping this from me." He moved forward, kicking through branches until he stood before her, his palm immediately stretching possessively over Alyss's stomach. "Do not dare suggest I am only here to do the honorable thing. We both know I'm not honorable."

"Then why are you here, Malcolm Sinclair?" The words trembled from her lips, so unlike her usual tart way of speaking.

"I'm kidnapping you. This time for real. I won't be asking for any ransom either." He grabbed her by the arms and pressed a hard, hurried kiss to her lips.

"You won't?"

"I love you, Alyss. Surely, you realize it."

A small sound left her. Like a wounded bird.

"You don't have to say it back. To you, love means something terrifying. But I'll prove to you that it is not. And one day, you can tell me what is in your heart. So until then, I will say it for both of us."

Alyss sobbed, tears running down her cheeks. She grabbed at his coat. "Forgive me. Malcolm. Please."

"I will, little fairy. Eventually." He kissed her again. "But right now, we need to get on with the kidnapping. I can't have your bullfrog chasing us down."

She looked up at him and brushed away a tear. "Is this a formal proposal of marriage, Mr. Sinclair?"

"In a manner of speaking. A formal proposal allows you the option to refuse." Alyss yelped as he picked her up and threw her over his shoulder. Strolling to the gate at the back of the garden, he said, "I assure you, this kidnapping will end in a marriage."

"Would you like me to struggle? Present some sort of a challenge?" she said, her voice muffled against his back.

"If you like. It might make things more realistic."

The hum of her laughter vibrated along his skin as she playfully swatted at him. Once they left the garden and shut the gate she said, "Where are we going?"

Malcolm smiled and started humming as he approached the carriage. "You'll see."

ALYSS ROLLED OVER, body sinking into the mattress of the bed at Buckmore's cottage. Or at least, what had been Buckmore's cottage. Malcolm had purchased it. He'd left a carefully worded letter for Buckmore before coming for Alyss, stating his intention along with the name of the Sinclair family solicitor who would be forwarding payment.

Just as with Alyss, Buckmore had not been given the opportunity to refuse.

They'd been here for over a fortnight while various messengers blew back and forth from London, which Patchahoo, the Sinclair family's solicitor, delivered in person. He was the only one who knew exactly where Alyss and Malcolm were. She hadn't even told Elizabeth. They'd been wed yesterday, a rushed affair witnessed only by Patchahoo, but Alyss didn't mind.

Uncle Richard had managed to smooth things over with Mr. Clinton. No easy task. Her uncle wasn't happy with her at present, if only because it left him to deal with Clinton. Elizabeth, in her letter to Alyss, had been overjoyed, especially at her part in bringing Alyss and Malcolm together. At the end of the week, they would return to London and start their new life together and meet Malcolm's family of which she was the latest, scandalous member.

The covers moved, shifting sinuously as Malcolm's body moved down, his breath teasing against her stomach and ribs. His teeth grazed along her hip, fingers moving between her thighs.

"Good morning, Mrs. Sinclair."

Alyss's legs splayed open, feeling the chafe of his short beard against her inner thigh. She'd decided to allow him to keep it, though she didn't care for facial hair in the least.

"Good morning, husband." She smiled and flipped back the blanket to gaze down at him.

"I like the sound of that," Malcolm growled, wedging himself between her thighs. "I don't recall, did we consummate our marriage?"

Alyss shrugged. "My memory fails. Perhaps I had too much brandy with the vicar." She was blissfully happy. So filled with joy at knowing the beautiful man loved her. They'd spent hours laying in the field behind the cottage, watching the clouds and discussing the future. Alyss had told Malcolm everything. The desert. Her father. The horrible day of her mother's death. And he, in turn, had explained about Dunnings.

Alyss and her parasol couldn't wait to officially become acquainted with Lady Longwood.

"I must ensure then, that this marriage is legal," Malcolm laughed. "Patchahoo would insist."

EPILOGUE

A LYSS HELD TIGHT to Malcolm's hand as he led her into the white stone three-story residence. The home was situated on a quiet street, close to Emerson House, but far enough to be discreet and give them privacy. She'd often wondered about this house, which had stood vacant, on and off, for years. With good reason.

"What do you think?" he asked, looking around the foyer. "Needs paint and plaster. I think most of the furnishings are decades old."

She sidestepped a small mountain of mouse droppings, gazing up at the windows, which were tall and wide but in need of a good cleaning. "I suppose it's difficult to sell a house everyone claims is haunted. Pity you couldn't find a home with fairies."

"I thought ghastly specters to be a good compromise," he winked at her. "Also, it makes us sound rather fearless, doesn't it? Living in a house with ghosts?"

"The only one in your family the least excited was Odessa. She'll be here every day trying to speak to the dead."

"Probably," Malcolm shrugged and walked to a pair of doors, flinging them open. "This will serve as my offices." He nodded at the far corner where a door was discernable through a stack of old furniture. "That will be the entrance for prospective clients. They won't come to the front door. I'll have to find someone like Holly to run the household."

"I believe Tamsin has someone in mind. Holly apparently has a younger brother."

"Splendid. Now these doors," he pointed to the ones they'd just come through. "Will lock from the outside so no one gets curious and wanders about our home. And," Malcolm dragged her toward the back of the house. "There's a garden. An enormous one. You can sit out there and go over reports and such in the sunshine."

Alyss followed him outside, wobbling just slightly on the steps.

Malcolm caught her deftly with a laugh. "Careful, my love."

"I am less than graceful these days." She looked over the mound of her stomach. "Odessa thinks it might be twins." Alyss was rather enormous.

"Odessa wants it to be twins. She finds the idea to be fascinating. Always asking if Drew and I can send messages to each other from London to Lincolnshire with our minds." He shook his head, glancing at her rounded form. "Twins do run in the family. Did I mention that the murders took place in the garden? Mr. Shepherd disposed of his wife just over there." He pointed to a barren patch of earth. "Not sure what happened to the butler."

Supposedly, Mrs. Shepherd and the butler, her lover, were the ghosts in question. Neighbors claimed to see them wandering about the gardens or waving from one of the windows.

Honestly, why would a ghost wave to anyone?

"Then how lovely you wish me to spend time out here. You should be careful of your words, husband." Alyss stepped carefully forward. "Perhaps another murder will occur in this house," teased. "If you don't behave, Malcolm Sinclair."

"Oh, I haven't forgotten your teeth and claws." He gave her a heated stare. "The marks on my back are testament to your viciousness."

Alyss had the decency to blush as she surveyed the weeds littering the flower beds. Perhaps it was her condition, but her physical needs had only intensified in the last few months. "It was only a small bite, Malcolm."

"You drew blood." He tugged at her hand. "But I don't mind."

He hadn't. Alyss was sure half the servants at Emerson House heard them. "Holly wouldn't look me in the eye at breakfast. And I think we broke the bed."

"Shoddy workmanship. Well, what do you think?"

Malcolm was good at several things. Weaponry. Fighting. But also surveillance. Breaking into homes. Gathering information. Putting what he collected together to draw the correct conclusion. He had read about a former soldier in France who had opened a private investigation service and decided to follow his example. Discreetly. Malcolm declared himself the "gentleman's investigator." Every title in London flocked to him.

Now, that word had gotten out, Malcolm had more clients than he could handle alone. He would need to hire an associate. Alyss compiled his reports, often pointing out clues he'd missed or she did her own surveillance, gathering information at her endless rounds of charitable luncheons, but soon, she would be busy with other things.

"I love it," Alyss said. "I think it's perfect. Ghosts and all. Oh." She pressed his hand to her stomach. "Do you feel that?"

Malcolm leaned over, pressing a kiss to the spot.

Love, as it turned out, was terrifying. But well worth every minute. She'd never actually said the words, but here, in this half-dead garden, surrounded by ghosts and possibly a fairy or two, and the child they'd made kicking away in her stomach, Alyss was overwhelmed. There were times she almost wanted to thank Buckmore for being such a loathsome creature, else she would not have Malcolm.

"I love you, Malcolm Sinclair." She took his fingers and squeezed. A tear slipped from one eye as she took in his beloved face. "I love you."

He pressed a kiss to her lips. "Don't cry, Alyss. I know."

About the Author

Kathleen Ayers is the bestselling author of steamy Regency and Victorian romance. She's been a hopeful romantic and romance reader since buying Sweet Savage Love at a garage sale when she was fourteen while her mother was busy looking at antique animal planters. She has a weakness for tortured, witty alpha males who can't help falling for intelligent, sassy heroines.

A Texas transplant (from Pennsylvania) Kathleen spends most of her summers attempting to grow tomatoes (a wasted effort) and floating in her backyard pool with her two dogs, husband and son. When not writing she likes to visit her "happy place" (Newport, RI.), wine bars, make homemade pizza on the grill, and perfect her charcuterie board skills. Visit her at www.kathleenayers.com.